MIDNIGHT PREDATOR

AMELIA ATWATER-RHODES

DELACORTE PRESS

Published by
Delacorte Press
an imprint of
Random House Children's Books
a division of Random House, Inc.
1540 Broadway
New York, New York 10036

Visit us on the Web! www.randomhouse.com/teens
Educators and librarians, for a variety of teaching tools, visit us at
www.randomhouse.com/teachers

Cataloging-in-Publication Data is available from the Library of Congress.
ISBN: 0-385-32794-3

The text of this book is set in 12-point Cochin.

Manufactured in the United States of America

May 2002

10 9 8 7 6 5 4 3

BTP

She made a little shadow-hidden grave,
    The day Faith died;
Therein she laid it, heard the clod's sick fall,
    And smiled aside —
"If less I ask," tear-blind, she mocked, "I may
    Be less denied."

She set a rose to blossom in her hair,
    The day Faith died —
"Now glad," she said, "and free at last, I go,
    And life is wide."
But through long nights she stared into the dark,
    And knew she lied.

The Dead Faith
Fannie Heaslip Lea

CHAPTER I

SOME PEOPLE USE THINGS; they destroy. You're a creator, a builder. The words came unbidden to her mind, completely inappropriate at the moment.

Distracted by the memory, Turquoise missed a block. She hissed in pain as the knife cut deep into the meaty underside of her arm. She caught her attacker's wrist and twisted, sending the young woman attached sprawling to the ground, as her father's words faded from her mind. Once, they might have been right, but now, they could not have been further from the truth.

The woman Turquoise was fighting wasn't

clumsy for long. In a near-blur of burgundy hair and black leather, Ravyn Aniketos sprang to her feet.

Turquoise rolled her shoulders, trying to work out the kinks in them, and blinked quickly to clear her tired eyes. This match had been going on for too long. She was bleeding from where Ravyn's knife had sliced through her arm, and she could feel the warm, sticky drip of blood down her back from a second wound on her left shoulder. Ravyn's black leather pants had been slit open in the thigh, and she had a shallow wound low on her jaw, which would probably heal without scarring.

Earlier, there had been other combatants; most slunk out the back door, defeated, within the first few minutes.

The fight was a competition of stealth and hunting ability. In near darkness, the competitors found and marked one another—a quick knife slice, just enough to draw blood. If a hunter was marked three times, he or she was out of the running. Turquoise was pleased to have lasted so long, but only victory would satisfy her pride. Ravyn likely felt the same. The next one of them to land a blow would win, becoming the leader of Crimson, the most elite unit of the Bruja guilds.

Somewhere in the building, a clock struck, once, twice . . .

Turquoise lost track of the clock's tones as she struck again. Ravyn cursed as the blade narrowly missed her stomach, and Turquoise barely managed to evade an answering strike to her cheek.

They were both getting tired, and tired quickly became clumsy. Only the fact that they had both been fighting for hours kept them evenly matched.

The clock finished its song, and left the room in eerie silence, broken only by the ragged, heavy breathing as the two fought.

"Ravyn. Turquoise."

Turquoise slid a fraction of her attention to the voice but did not allow her gaze to leave Ravyn.

"Sheathe your weapons," Bruja's leader, Sarta, instructed. Someone flipped the switch and both fighters blinked against the sudden light. "I have a feeling that this competition could go on for days if I let it," she announced, "but Bruja law does call for a limit."

Ravyn licked the blade of her knife clean, her cranberry-colored gaze resting on Turquoise all the while, as if daring her to react. Ravyn had no fetish for blood, and she professed to hate vampires, but she did love to give a show.

"Well, Sarta, if you're going to call a halt to our fun, do you also plan to name a winner?" Ravyn was still panting slightly, but not enough to affect the smooth drawl in her voice.

Turquoise wiped her own blade on the leg of her ruined jeans. She didn't speak yet, preferring to catch her breath. If it was ten now, then she and Ravyn had been sparring for almost five hours. This fight had begun at sunrise.

Five hours, and they were left in a draw. Turquoise's muscles ached with fatigue, but she would rather have finished this than stopped now. She wanted the title.

Crimson. It was the most elite of the three Bruja guilds. Cold-blooded as snakes and vicious as hyenas, members of Bruja were the best predators in existence. To be recognized as the guild's leader would fulfill the promise

Turquoise had once made. She had sworn that no one would ever mistake her for prey again. If that meant abandoning a few of the social mores of the daylight world, as Bruja members so frequently did, so be it.

The leader of Crimson was second only to Sarta, the leader of all three Bruja guilds. Turquoise had trained and fought and competed for the position. She knew she was the best Crimson had. She could out-stalk and out-fight any vampire and had, many times. She would win this title, whatever it took.

"Rematch," Sarta said simply. "Onyx and Frost still need to compete today. You two are obviously matched evenly with daggers, but a Bruja member needs to be able to use any weapon at his or her command." She paused for dramatic effect. "A tie is decided in a private duel, one month after Challenge, witnessed only by the other leaders. The weapon is decided by the member who has been in the guild the longest—in this case, Ravyn—and the bout goes to third blood."

Ravyn sighed, looking at Turquoise past burgundy lashes. "In one month, and I choose the weapon. In that case . . ." She walked around the room, examining the walls, which were decorated with weapons of all sizes, all shapes, and all designs.

She paused to run a finger down the blade of a broadsword, but then shook her head and moved on. She glanced at the crossbows, but they were the traditional weapon of Crimson's sister guild, Onyx—not appropriate for a Crimson duel. She passed foils, epées, and sabers, and did not even pause to glance at the thick wooden staves.

Finally, she pulled down two leather whips, and cracked one expertly. "I choose these."

Ravyn tossed one of them to Turquoise with a sly grin, and Turquoise almost let it fall to the ground before reflex made her catch the handle. Of the entire selection of weapons in the Bruja hall, the whip was the only one she hated. Ravyn could not have made a better choice.

"Turquoise, do you accept the challenge?" Sarta asked.

"I accept." She was grateful that her voice stayed even. She hated whips. She could use one if she needed to, but not with any precision.

"Then get out of here," Sarta ordered. "Come back the day of the next full moon. The match will begin at sunrise."

Turquoise nodded, then turned her back to Sarta and Ravyn, and stalked as gracefully as she could from the fighting floor.

She paused next to the cork assignment board, collecting herself before she left the halls.

Ravyn had come up behind her to look at the board. Turquoise's instincts told her to leave. Ravyn, like all Bruja members, was not someone Turquoise trusted at her back. So of course she forced herself to stay and read the notices.

Turquoise ignored most of the posts. She was a mercenary, but she had standards, and she preferred vampires as her prey. There were numbers up on a couple of shape-shifters, but none sounded interesting. Besides, Turquoise was still a little wary of putting a knife in something that breathed and bled like a human, even if it did grow fur, scales, or feathers occasionally.

The rest of the posts she tried to avoid reading. She liked to think no amount of money was worth stalking human targets, but she knew most Bruja members dis-agreed. Some argued that cowardice kept her from hunting her own kind. When Turquoise had first joined Bruja, the older members had taken bets on how long it would take her to make her first human kill.

They were still waiting.

Turquoise finally slipped away from the hall, stretching as she shouldered open the door to the bright outside.

A stranger, a young woman no more than twenty-five years old, was waiting for her. She held up her hands to show she was un-armed. "Turquoise Draka?" she inquired. Her voice was polished, the accent vaguely English.

Turquoise nodded cautiously. Her eyes had adjusted to the sunlight now, and she sized up this woman. She looked fairly harm-less, with brown hair pulled back in an ele-gant twist, and wearing a cream business suit over a chocolate-colored blouse. A leather folio leaned against the wall beside her.

However, the woman's heels made no sound on the stone walk as she approached, and even in the mid-June heat, her face showed no hint of sweat. Turquoise trusted her ability to recognize a vampire on sight, but just because this woman was not a bloodsucker did not mean she was human.

"Ah, and here is Ravyn Aniketos," the woman called, as Ravyn slipped tiredly through the door. Though she must still have been sunblind, Ravyn drew a dagger instantly upon hearing her name.

Ravyn and Turquoise exchanged a look, and a mental shrug passed between them. Although they were enemies at times, rivals for power always, they were both intelligent enough to put their differences aside if confronted by a threat. Vampire, witch, shapeshifter, or human, this woman didn't stand a chance if her intentions were less than friendly.

"Something I can help you with?" Turquoise inquired warily.

"Yes. My name is Jillian Red." The name had the sound of a pseudonym. Jillian extended her hand, but did not seem surprised when no one reached out to shake it. "I have been following your careers for about a year now. You both hold quite impressive ranks, and have shown a certain rancor toward a breed I am not too fond of myself."

Bored already, Turquoise assumed the woman's lengthy speech was just winding toward another job.

Ravyn had actually started to walk away. Turquoise debated doing the same, but was stopped by the woman's next words.

"You both show a certain promise in your history, namely, some unpleasant experiences with the trade."

Turquoise did not need to ask which trade. From the sudden tension that pulsed through Ravyn's body as she turned back, she had understood the words just as well.

"And what do you know of our history?" Ravyn asked, voice silky as a black widow's thread.

Jillian Red sighed. "You, Ravyn, first came to vampiric attention when you were fifteen, and were brought into the trade by a low-power mercenary named Jared. You were lucky enough to avoid the professional slave traders, but unlucky enough—"

Ravyn shook her head, sending silky cranberry hair shuddering about her shoulders. "This is unnecessary."

"Unlucky enough," Jillian continued, "to be in the midst of vampires who respected

Jared's claim of ownership and because of it would not come to your aid no matter how much they disapproved of his treatment of you."

Ravyn was by this point visibly simmering, her frame so rigid Turquoise suspected bone and sinew would shatter if the hunter tried to move.

"Shortly after he acquired you, Jared was found dead," Jillian finished, "and about a week after that, you entered Crimson."

"What is the job?" Ravyn snapped.

"Shall we find some place to sit and discuss the particulars?" Jillian suggested. "Even if you choose not to accept my offer, which I doubt, you will be well-paid for your time."

"Lead the way," Turquoise said, when Ravyn did not immediately speak. If this woman knew as much about Turquoise's history as she did about Ravyn's, that knowledge could make her inconvenient, if not dangerous. It would not hurt to learn what she wanted.

CHAPTER 2

FIFTEEN MINUTES LATER, they were gathered around a small table in Jillian Red's hotel room, looking at pictures the woman drew out of her briefcase.

"This is a copy of a painting made back in 1690," their host explained as she placed the first print on the table. "I don't suppose either of you recognizes it?"

The painting focused on an intimidating building, the outside walls of which were painted black with an abstract design in red. The grounds maintained the pattern with burgundy-leafed ground cover that had been carefully planted around black stone. A path of white slate wound sinuously up to the door, which was flanked by lushly growing roses. The blooms, which had been carefully depicted by the artist, were pure black.

The painting looked familiar, but Turquoise could not place it.

Jillian Red launched into a history lesson. "In the early sixteen hundreds two sisters, vampires both, founded an empire they called Midnight. This building was the heart, the symbol so to speak, of their power. They were less than five hundred years old, young compared to most of their kind, but they both were ruthless, and more organized than their elders; their determination allowed them to take control swiftly."

Jillian glanced at the white stucco ceiling, and continued, "Jeshickah, the younger of the two sisters, was the absolute ruler of Midnight. For a few hundred years, she controlled nearly all the vampires, the shapeshifters, and the witches. As for the humans . . . they were little more than cattle. If a human was sold into Midnight, that was the end."

"You keep saying Midnight *was*," Turquoise thought aloud, anxious to get to the present and learn what the job was. She was not a fan of history, and she already knew more about the vampiric slave trade than she cared to. "What is it now?"

"I'll get there," Jillian chastised. "In the early eighteen hundreds, Midnight was destroyed by a group of older, stronger vampires. The building was leveled, and every living creature caught inside was killed. Of course the vampires survived, but with the property and slaves lost, the empire lost its heart, and the rival power was able to take control.

"The new leaders banned the slave trade—they did not approve of caged meat—but as you two have witnessed, the laws have slackened over time. The original vampires of Midnight were able to pick up the trade again." Jillian sighed. "That might have been bad enough, but . . ." She reached into her briefcase again, and this time pulled out a glossy eight-by-ten photograph.

"This was sent to me a few days ago."

The photo did not need to be explained. Someone had rebuilt Midnight.

"The trade has been pulled together by a new master, one of the trainers from the original Midnight. My employer, who wishes to remain anonymous, was unconcerned about Midnight's revival until recently, when the original founder returned. With the groundwork already in place, Jeshickah is expressing an interest in taking charge again. My employer would like that threat eliminated.

"The offer for Jeshickah's death is a half million to each of you, with that much again to split as you wish if the job is done within the next week. I am only the agent, and have only been contacted via writing, so I can offer little more information than I have given you. Are you interested?"

"Why hire two Bruja to go after one leech? It's a waste of money," Ravyn asked, the question both practical and suspicious. An anonymous employer could mean many things. It could be he had no intention of paying, or more likely it meant that he feared his target.

"My employer has a wish to have this job over quickly," Jillian answered. "Hiring two of you is insurance. If one of you does not succeed, the other might."

In other words, they were expendable,

and Jillian's anonymous employer wanted to have a backup in case one of them got killed. Someone either didn't have much faith in Bruja abilities, or had more information than Turquoise and Ravyn were receiving.

"Sounds fun," Ravyn acknowledged, scraping away a speck of blood she had just noticed on one of her burgundy nails. "With luck, we won't have to worry about the re-match, either," she added to Turquoise.

Turquoise shrugged. This job was worth too much to turn her back on. Besides, she had never met a vampire she couldn't beat. "You say get inside," she inquired, tacitly accepting Jillian's terms. "How?"

"That's one of the reasons the job isn't cheap," Jillian said, a slight smile on her face. "You're on your own to get into Midnight. You'll have to use any means necessary, Turquoise."

Turquoise knew what Jillian was hinting at. "I need to make a call."

An hour later, Turquoise found herself in yet another hotel room, this time with a fairly attractive, dark-skinned gentleman three or four hundred years old. It was hard to tell exactly, since in appearance he was twenty-five at the most. As broaching the topic of any vampire's past could be danger-ous at best, Turquoise had never asked.

"Milady Turquoise," he greeted.

"Nathaniel, always nice to see you," she responded sincerely. Nathaniel was a vam-pire, true, and that was not his only flaw; he was also a mercenary and an assassin, as ne-cessity dictated. However, since Turquoise also fit most of those descriptions, she did not hold Nathaniel's profession against him.

Luckily, Nathaniel's line thirsted more for money than for blood. If anyone thought it strange that a vampire and a human had a close business relationship, no one had spo-ken of it. Nathaniel had taught Turquoise most of what she knew. He had taught her what a mercenary was, the value of her tal-ents—among them hunting—and most im-portantly, where to find buyers for the skills she was willing to sell. He had also once saved her life, not to mention her sanity.

"I don't suppose this is a social call," Nathaniel stated. "You on a job?"

She nodded, debating how much she needed to tell him. Though he would offer her a chance to buy his silence, Nathaniel would be willing and able to sell any information she gave him.

"I need to get myself and another woman into Midnight." The slight widening of Nathaniel's eyes was the only sign that she had surprised him. "And I need to do it without getting tied up or beaten bloody."

Nathaniel sighed and leaned back against the wall. "You don't ask for much, do you, Turquoise?" he said with heavy sarcasm. "Are you trying to get yourself killed?"

She frowned at the tone of his voice. It was unlike Nathaniel to object to anything someone else was doing, especially if he was likely to get paid for it.

"Will you get us in?"

"I could sell you in," Nathaniel responded bluntly. His gaze flickered down and up her body, a critical sizing up. "You would fetch a high number, I'm sure. Attractive, healthy, strong, intelligent . . . or I thought you were. Are you really so anxious to sell yourself back into slavery, Turquoise?"

No. She had been in once; she had no desire to return. However, to return with a knife, as an experienced hunter, was a great deal different than returning unarmed, as the innocent she had once been.

"Is there any other way?"

Nathaniel shook his head, and inventoried her price in a cool tone that sent shivers down her spine. "The scars on your arms will lessen your value by a couple hundred. Unless you would like me to offer you to Daryl? He would pay dearly."

She recoiled as Nathaniel said her once-master's name.

Gathering her pride, she stated, "If he's involved in Midnight, I'm definitely going in. He's deserved a knife for a long time."

"You weren't always so tough, Turquoise," Nathaniel said softly. He had been the one who had given her the name Turquoise Draka, a new identity to replace the one Lord Daryl had destroyed. He had provided her with contacts to Bruja, and had taught her about fighting back instead of cowering. He had never told her why, and she had never asked. "I've seen you pull stunts that left me wondering if you had a death wish. You push yourself hard enough to kill a weaker human, and accept jobs that should be suicide missions just to prove you can handle them."

She shrugged, and found that her shoulders were painfully tight. "I've never lost," she pointed out. "And I've never known you to argue with me before."

Nathaniel just sighed. "It's your life," he finally relented. "You know the slave trade better than most freeblood humans will ever imagine it."

He paused, and then named his price. "Forty thousand, in advance. And I'll take whatever I can get for selling the two of you. I haven't dealt in flesh since the old Midnight was destroyed, but I've had enough pressure to return to it that my selling a couple of humans for a profit won't surprise anyone. Deal, milady?" Nathaniel had returned to his usual cool composure, and the familiar tone helped soothe her jangled nerves.

She nodded. "Deal."

"Shall we find your companion?"

Again she nodded. They walked down the hall to the room where Ravyn and Jillian were waiting.

A few paces from the doorway to Jillian Red's hotel room, she asked, "Why does Midnight scare you so much?" It was not a polite question. Asking any vampire about his fear was like asking a parent why his child was diseased.

She half-expected him to clam up, but instead he leveled a dark gaze in her direction.

Then he looked away, flashing a handsome smile at some memory as he stepped toward the doorway. "Because I was part of it once," he answered. "I know Midnight and the woman who once ran it better than you could ever imagine; I understand what went on inside. And while I'm not nearly so mad as the people I surround myself with, I seem to have a rather unprofessional desire not to see you kill yourself."

Turquoise was still trying to decide whether that last bit was an insult or a compliment when Nathaniel knocked on Jillian Red's door.

CHAPTER 3

RAVYN HAD SEEMED to be thoroughly amused when she learned of the masquerade she would have to play in order to earn her money, but as they went over the finer points of slavery at a Chinese restaurant along the way, she became decidedly less delighted.

Nathaniel spoke between sips of tea and polite bites of sesame chicken. Turquoise wondered whether he liked the taste, or was just willing to eat so they would look normal, as the vampire certainly did not need the human food.

He explained calmly, "If you don't want to be bound and thrown into a cell, you're going to need to pass for a tamed slave. No trainer will believe you are broken, but if you're careful, he might be satisfied that you're smart enough to be obedient. I've heard that Midnight isn't as brutal to its slaves as it once was, so a bit of servility should buy you enough time for your job." For Ravyn's benefit, he elaborated. "Your master is more than your owner—he is your life, the only thing that matters. Nothing comes before his wishes. What he says, you do, without hesitation. Until you're sold, that master is me. When we get to Midnight, keep your eyes on me. If someone tells you to do something, look to me. If someone asks you a question, look to me. Once you're sold, the same applies to whoever your new owner is. A slave isn't supposed to think; she just obeys.

"Never address the vampires by name unless given permission to do so. I know of very few who would hesitate to give a slave a beating if she forgot a title. In general, address any of my kind as 'milady' or 'milord' until told otherwise."

He paused. "The present Master of Midnight is named Jaguar. He was a trainer in the original Midnight—one of the best. Avoid him as well as you can, because he'll see through your act quickly."

"Tell us about this Midnight," Turquoise pressed, when Nathaniel paused again.

"I have avoided this new Midnight so far, but I knew the old one too well," Nathaniel answered. "I've seen humans bred like cattle, beaten bloody for meaningless trifles. Worse, I've seen freeborn humans as strong willed as you two reduced to the servility of well-trained pets." He raised his gaze to meet first Ravyn's then Turquoise's, scanning each of their expressions. "I've been told that Jaguar is changing some of the rules. People have been objecting that he's too gentle with humans now, but no one with the power to overthrow him has bothered to do so. Don't let his seeming kindness fool you. After Jeshickah, Jaguar was the most vicious trainer in Midnight. Even if he has somehow gained a set of morals, old habits die hard.

"Once I sell you in, you're on your own. None of Midnight's followers will go against a claim of ownership, so even if you want to pay a mercenary for help escaping, he won't be able to take you out."

Nathaniel was giving them one more warning. He had been the one to remove Turquoise from her first master's possession, but only after Lord Daryl had thrown her away in a rage and ordered the mercenary to take her.

"It won't be a problem," Ravyn replied, though Turquoise could hear strain in her voice. According to Jillian's recital, Ravyn had found herself once before in the uncomfortable situation Nathaniel was describing. The hunter was putting forward a brave front. "Tell us more about this Jeshickah you mentioned."

"Jeshickah . . ." Nathaniel shook his head. "She gathered her trainers and taught them their trade. She picked the slaves who would be bred and the slaves who would be culled. After her Midnight was destroyed, she withdrew from vampire society." He continued, "So far, she doesn't seem to be involved with Jaguar's project. Jaguar was Jeshickah's favorite—brutal, and perfectly obedient to her. It isn't surprising that he would attempt to re-create the environment in which he had power." He turned to describing the trainer instead, leaving Turquoise unable to press about Jeshickah without revealing that she was their target. "Don't trust Jaguar, and don't irritate him unless you are willing to take a beating for it. It takes a lot to get his temper riled, but once it is, you're in trouble. In general, don't give him any reason to touch you, especially in anger, but don't fight him if he does. *Never* raise a hand against a trainer, not unless you know you can kill him."

"Is he usually armed?" Turquoise asked the question out of habit. Both hunters were leaving their weapons behind; there would be no way to explain if someone noticed they were carrying when they entered Midnight. However, there were always ways to find weaponry, especially if one's prey was wearing it.

"Jaguar rarely uses a knife," Nathaniel answered. "He favors a nine-foot leather whip, which he is an expert with. I've seen him slice open the arm of another vampire, then pull a bird unharmed from the air with the back snap."

Ravyn shook her head, sipping her water in contemplation. Turquoise found that burgundy gaze risen to meet her own. "Something wrong, Turquoise?" she drawled. "You look a bit pale."

"Just annoyed," she answered briskly, forcing her composure to return. Knives, crossbows, swords, staves . . . why did it have to be a whip?

It's practical. The voice in her memory was Lord Daryl's, answering that question, asked three years earlier. *A knife is more likely to scar, or do greater harm than intended. It is easier to establish discipline with a more versatile weapon.*

Lord Daryl had been able to snap a whip softly enough to sting the flesh, or hard enough to draw blood, depending on his mood.

Nathaniel's gaze met hers across the table; he no doubt knew what she was thinking. Then he looked away, his eyes rising to flirt with the waitress who had just returned to refill their water glasses.

As soon as she was gone, Nathaniel continued. "Turquoise, you might want to go back to using your birth name; it will make it easier to convince anyone you see that you have been bounced around inside the trade the last few years. Either way, don't use Turquoise Draka—it's too easy to trace.

Ravyn, how likely are you to be recognized?"

Ravyn shook her head. "All the vampires I've ever known are dead." Nathaniel gave her a look that said he heard both the implied threat and the lie, but Ravyn volunteered nothing more.

Nathaniel took another sip of tea. He held the liquid in his mouth a few moments, as if thinking of something else. "I normally don't make a point of arguing the plans of someone who is paying me, but you both know this is insanity, don't you?"

"Insanity makes the rivers flow," Ravyn replied nonsensically.

"Any more advice you're willing to share?" Turquoise asked, ignoring Ravyn as well as she could. She bit back a yawn, and then frowned at her watch. It was only noon. Grudgingly, she admitted to herself that even she had limits. She had been up since three in the morning, and had spent much of the time fighting Ravyn. Still, there was enough adrenaline left in her system that she had expected to be wired until next Tuesday.

Nathaniel paused. "None that's going to

mean much to you. With luck, you won't have any trouble dealing with Jaguar. He's probably stronger than the vampires you've faced before, but he's weak compared to Jeshickah. If Jeshickah or Gabriel are there, pray you don't run into either of them."

Ravyn's gaze snapped up from what had been a sleepy-looking contemplation of her chopsticks when she heard the second name.

"Something wrong?" Nathaniel inquired.

She shook her head. A frown crossed her brow briefly, and Turquoise saw her stifle a yawn. As always, the yawn was contagious.

The waitress had returned with their check. By the time Nathaniel had taken the appropriate number of bills from his wallet, Turquoise was taking deep breaths in an attempt to keep awake.

One foot in front of the other, Turquoise ordered herself as she followed Nathaniel to the car. He opened the two passenger-side doors before walking around to the driver's side. The passenger's bucket seat sank beneath Turquoise invitingly.

Turquoise was nearly unconscious before she turned her doubling vision on Nathaniel.

You drugged us? It took two tries to form the thought coherently, and then her lips seemed too dry to say it aloud.

Sleep, Turquoise, Nathaniel returned, speaking with his mind as he started the car. *It's a long drive to Midnight, and there's no reason for you to know the way.*

But . . .

Sleep.

CHAPTER 4

THERE WERE THREE cartoon characters to choose from, though of course the best ones were on the square bandages and the tiny ones, the ones no one ever had a use for.

"There, all patched up," Cathy announced. "You take care of Bert for me," she commanded. The eight-year-old boy grinned, any pain from the scrape on his shin forgotten in the swath of Sesame Street bandages, and kissed his sister on the cheek before hopping down.

Tommy scampered off about the time that her dad descended the stairs. "That boy gets into more trouble in one afternoon . . ." He shook his head, still smiling. "He's lucky to have you. Most fifteen-

year-old girls have better things to do than take care of their brothers."

Cathy shrugged. It sounded like Mr. Minate was about to launch into another of his inspirational talks.

"Honestly." Right on cue. "Some people only care about themselves. They use things; they destroy. You're . . . you're a creator, a builder. A healer, not a user."

Cathy shook off the words using the traditional "nod and smile" approach. Her father seemed to realize he had descended into the depths of hokey advice again, and gave her an impulsive hug. "Don't let anyone change you, Cathy."

The dream crumbled, and Turquoise wrenched herself away from sleep, trying to gather her bearings. *You are not that innocent girl anymore. You are Turquoise Draka, a high-ranking member of Crimson, and a vampire hunter—one of the best.* She pushed the memories away.

She was on a job. Memories had no place here.

She was sprawled across the passenger seat of Nathaniel's car, with a kink in her back where someone seemed to have tied the muscles into a square knot. She rotated her shoulders, cautiously peering out the car's window as she pushed the remnants of her dream away.

They were parked at a gas station. Through the window, she could see Nathaniel speaking to the cashier, an attractive young woman.

Flirt, Turquoise thought without bitterness, as she saw the cashier leaning forward, giving her customer an excellent view. Her hand lingered, fingers brushing over Nathaniel's as she handed him his change.

Turquoise heard Ravyn starting to come to, as she waited for Nathaniel to get back in the car so she could grill him. It was dusk already; she wanted to know when they would arrive in Midnight.

She had just reached for her door handle, ready to confront the vampire, when she saw how the cashier's flirting had paid off.

Nathaniel was holding the girl gently, almost in an embrace, one arm around her waist and his other hand on the back of her arched neck.

Turquoise stretched, turning away from the scene, and then fumbled with the radio dial for a few seconds, finding only static. Nathaniel was too discreet to kill the girl, and he had to feed sometime.

Ravyn grumbled a curse. "What the hell?" she snarled. "That—"

"We didn't pay him to tell us where Midnight was," Turquoise interrupted the other hunter. She had worked with Nathaniel numerous times; she knew how he thought. "And most likely, someone is paying him not to give Midnight's location away."

Ravyn grumbled an insult that Turquoise pretended not to hear. "What's all the drama about this job? I've killed older bloodsuckers than this Jeshickah. She might have a bad rap, but that will all change once she's got a knife in her."

Turquoise did not respond except to shake her head. Nathaniel obviously did not know that Jeshickah was back. Jillian had said her return was very recent, and since Nathaniel had been avoiding Midnight, it was not surprising that his information was out of date. However, it was always worrisome when a prime source of information was wrong.

She sat back, forcing herself to relax. She

could plan once she knew the score; until then, worrying about details was pointless.

Ravyn continued to grumble as Nathaniel bid the cashier adieu. She sank groggily to the floor, and the vampire returned to the car with a new bounce in his step.

Opening the door, he tossed a box of donuts and a soda at Turquoise, who took the drink gratefully; her mouth was dry as cotton. When Nathaniel offered one to Ravyn, the other hunter refused to do more than glare at the bottle.

"It's sealed," he assured her.

"No thank you."

"Suit yourself." He dropped the soda into the cup holder. "We're about ten minutes away from Midnight. If you want anything to eat—"

"No," Ravyn said again.

Nathaniel chuckled lightly, shaking his head. "Turquoise?"

She dug into the donuts. The drug had made her hungry, and who knew how often Midnight fed its humans?

Lost in her own thoughts, Turquoise still could not have missed the shift into

Midnight's territories. The hair rose on the back of her neck, and the skin of her arms tingled; she saw Ravyn shudder as they passed through the almost solid wall of magic.

"Midnight has always had witches on its payroll," Nathaniel informed them. "They keep unwanted pests from stumbling in."

They had driven on a single-lane road from a suburban town, through whatever veil Midnight's witches had put up, past a thick wall of oak and pine trees, and into a different world. It was dark by now, and even the full moon above was all but obliterated by the thick leaves of this unnatural forest.

"We're here."

Turquoise found herself looking at a menacing building that could only be Midnight. A path of white marble led from the gates of an imposing iron fence guarded by iron ravens to the opulent, carved doorway, around which black roses grew. Though the red ground cover was slightly less overgrown, the building had obviously been designed in imitation of the antique painting Turquoise had seen.

Nathaniel swore under his breath, driving

off the road to avoid an oncoming car. Sleek claret, the car all but screamed money.

Ravyn whistled, leaning forward in her seat. "Who's got the Lamborghini?"

"Shut up." Nathaniel's voice was crisp. He pushed open his door, every movement tense—not quite fearful, but wary and displeased. "Stay here."

Turquoise caught his eye, but Nathaniel avoided her gaze. Instead, he approached the woman who had just stepped out of the Lamborghini. Suede encased her long legs— tall, black boots that laced from ankle to mid-thigh over a pair of black pants. The archaic-style boots contrasted with the modern styling of her shirt, which was the burgundy color of an especially bad bruise.

"Nathaniel," she greeted. Her tone was not friendly, but neither was it openly threatening.

"I heard you had decided not to involve yourself with Jaguar's project here," Nathaniel returned, nodding in the general direction of Midnight's main building.

"That was my plan," she responded dryly, "but Jaguar's games here have recently ceased to amuse me."

"How so?"

"This place is a mockery." She shook her head in disgust, and then her gaze fell on Turquoise and Ravyn, who were waiting in the car. "That one looks familiar. . . ." Turquoise's heart stopped. She had not known her name, but she remembered this woman on sight. Mistress Jeshickah had been a frequent visitor to Turquoise's tormentor's home. She had been the only creature in the world Lord Daryl would admit to fearing. Belatedly, Turquoise realized where she had seen the painting of Midnight—also in Lord Daryl's manor, hanging on the wall of his office. However, Jeshickah's gaze had settled on Ravyn. "Jared's pet, wasn't she?"

"Perhaps." Nathaniel glanced at Ravyn absently. "But I don't recall anyone quite like her."

Throughout the exchange, Ravyn's gaze had remained on the car door. Her expression, however, she could not control.

"She's not broken," Jeshickah observed.

"Not quite," Nathaniel agreed. "I thought Jaguar might enjoy that. I was going to present the girls to him directly."

"There was a time when you would have

enjoyed them yourself," Jeshickah responded. Turquoise saw Nathaniel's expression cool to a blank, unreadable mask. The words had struck a nerve.

"Jaguar is much more qualified than I ever was," he answered.

Jeshickah growled a rather unflattering expletive under her breath. Aloud, she added, "The little cat had talent, but I'm afraid time has liquefied his brain. I think I'll come with you and see what he makes of this fine pair. Jaguar will certainly deal with their pride." She sighed, and with an air of regretful practicality, added, "Or he won't, and I'll tear out the bleeding heart he's developed and make him eat it." She said the last words brightly and with a smile as she led the way toward Midnight, not even bothering to glance back to see if Nathaniel had heeded her commands.

"You two, follow," Nathaniel ordered Turquoise and Ravyn. The tone was surprisingly similar to the one with which Jeshickah had spoken to him, and as the mercenary had obeyed, so did the hunters.

CHAPTER 5

JESHICKAH'S BOOT HEELS made a sharp *click* each time they struck the marble walk. Turquoise had to resist a wince at every strike; it was the kind of sound that would give a tic to anyone who had to listen to it for too long.

The imposing, carved door opened to reveal a young boy, probably no older than fourteen. He started to walk outside, and then froze when he saw Jeshickah. His aborted step turned into a stumble, at the end of which Turquoise flinched to hear the impact of the boy's knees on marble. He moved as if to stand, and then rethought the action.

Jeshickah regarded the boy as if he were a sickly dog.

"Can I help you, milady?" His voice was soft, and he kept his eyes carefully on the ground.

"Stand up and get out of the way," she suggested. Carefully, the boy rose to his feet and slid aside, still never raising his eyes. He waited for Jeshickah, Nathaniel, Ravyn, and Turquoise to pass before slinking after them.

"Mangy cur," Jeshickah growled under her breath. She ignored the boy, who was following them, and spoke only to Nathaniel. "His name is Eric. Jaguar treats him like a son, gives him free rein of the building and grounds, even lets him into town when he wants to go. The creature is obedient, but spoiled."

Jeshickah led the way to Midnight's interior, which was slightly less intimidating, but no less elegant. An oaken panel ran halfway up the wall, where it broke into a rich jade green. A carpet of oriental design covered the floor, soft and plush enough that Turquoise could feel it through her sneakers.

Near the end of the hall, Jeshickah

pushed open a door and let the party into a dimly lit room.

Long ago, Turquoise had learned that the most evil creatures in the world were frequently the most beautiful. The Master of Midnight was no exception.

Jaguar—and it could only be him—was sprawled on his back across a black leather couch, one hand beneath his head, with his eyes closed. His skin was the color of a deep, golden tan, and his hair was black, perfectly straight and long. When he stood, it would probably hang to his lower back. He was wearing soft, black pants that hugged a body that Turquoise tried valiantly not to stare at.

That was it—no shirt, no shoes, no jewelry. The whip Nathaniel had mentioned was curled on Jaguar's chest like a black viper. His hand resting on the handle reminded Turquoise of a child with a beloved stuffed animal.

As she paused in the doorway, the vampire's eyes fluttered open—black eyes, like obsidian, they seemed to reflect the light cast from the lamp in the corner. They lit on Jeshickah instantly, and the expression on his face snapped from sleepy contentment to wary aggression as he stood.

Turquoise expected the two to come to blows in the moment of silence that passed, but instead Jeshickah spoke. "Have a good nap, pet?" she purred.

It took obvious effort for Jaguar to ignore her as he spoke to Nathaniel. "These the girls you called me about?"

The tension that Turquoise had seen in Nathaniel the instant he had sighted Jeshickah's car was either gone or flawlessly hidden. He nodded, explaining, "They aren't perfectly broken, but they're smart enough not to give you any trouble. Besides that, they're both healthy and fairly attractive. There's some scarring on that one," Nathaniel continued, gesturing toward Turquoise, "mostly on her arms, but nothing unusual."

"Let me see." The command came from Jeshickah.

Nathaniel had prepared Turquoise for the inspection, and so she was wearing her only tank top, over which she had thrown a cotton shirt despite the August heat. She hesitantly removed her outer layer.

The scars had been hers for nearly three years; she had hidden them for nearly that long. With only the tank top, she felt half naked.

"Whip?" Jaguar asked, frowning at the semicircle of scarring around Turquoise's left wrist, a smooth pearl bracelet cut into her skin.

Turquoise felt the muscles between her shoulder blades tense, but she kept her eyes down. She had already concocted the story she could tell if asked about her past. Only Lord Daryl would be able to contradict her, and she counted on his pride to keep him from doing so if the opportunity arose.

"Her first trainer wasn't as careful as most," Nathaniel answered vaguely.

Jaguar seemed to accept the answer. "How much for the pair of them?"

Nathaniel was in his element now. He was a green-blooded mercenary. Any fondness he had for Turquoise or distaste he held for Jeshickah or Jaguar faded as soon as the question of money was raised.

Jeshickah forestalled any bartering. "Allow me, kitten. You need a few more toys around here." Jaguar's glare met the nickname, but Jeshickah had already turned away from him. "Nathaniel, shall we haggle in private while Jaguar gets to know his new acquisitions?"

Jeshickah wrapped an arm around Nathaniel's waist. They walked out together, but the contact did not appear friendly.

In the silence of their departure, tension began to drain from the room. Jaguar let out a slow breath. Vampires by nature did not need to breathe, but human habits died hard.

Without speaking, he walked around the two humans, a silent inspection. It occurred to Turquoise that they were lucky to have this job so shortly after Challenge. They both had plenty of bruises and new cuts, the absence of which would have been suspicious. Turquoise watched her new master as long as he was in her line of sight. Jaguar moved like his namesake, all grace and muscle. His black hair was a black pelt smooth against his skin.

"Names?" he asked finally.

"Audra." Turquoise understood Nathaniel's suggestion not to use the name Turquoise Draka—her name was well known as a vampire hunter's—but there was no power on Earth that could make her start using Catherine again. Catherine had been innocent, a child—defenseless prey. The memories of that girl's life, her family and friends, were bittersweet at best.

"Ravyn," the other hunter answered defiantly, stupidly ignoring all advice.

Jaguar gave no sign of recognizing the girl. Instead, he offered, "If you have questions, ask them now."

"Are there any rules we should know, sir?" Turquoise could not have managed to say "milord" or "master" without choking.

She knew the one general rule of slavery: Do whatever you are told to do. However, there were always household rules; there had been many of those in Lord Daryl's manor, most of which Turquoise had learned painfully.

"Eric will find you something to do. So long as you get your work done, you may go almost anywhere in the building. I suggest you avoid the west wing unless you plan on a little bloodletting. Beyond that, if a door is locked, you aren't welcome." Jaguar paused, considering. "I don't mind intelligent conversation, so feel free to speak as you wish to me. If you bother me, I will tell you to shut up; I don't feel the need to hit people for talking. Around others of my kind, hold your tongue. Most aren't as lenient as I am." These last words were accompanied by a glance through the door which Jeshickah had passed. "Understand?"

"Yes, sir," Turquoise answered. Ravyn echoed her assent, though her "sir" sounded like it was spit out through clenched teeth.

Jaguar gave the girls a sharp look. "You'll want to practice that for Jeshickah, but I'm not fond of titles. Jaguar will do just fine."

Ravyn nodded, her lips just barely curled into the edge of a smile.

"You'll find I give few orders, especially once you get an idea as to how this place is run. If you choose to do everything I say, fine."

"If?" Turquoise prompted. He was all but telling her that she could disobey him. "Since when has a slave had a choice?"

Jaguar laughed, a rich laugh that startled Turquoise with its warmth. "If you choose not to obey, I suppose we will discuss that then, won't we?"

Completely shocked by the lack of threat

in his words, Turquoise could not speak for a moment, during which Jaguar decided the conversation was over. "Eric, come here," he called. The boy who had avoided Jeshickah like a beaten dog entered the room confidently. He did not seem afraid of Jaguar.

"Eric, get these two situated, and find something to keep them busy. I have other work I need to get done." With the words, Jaguar effortlessly changed from what for a moment had seemed like companionable bantering, back to the arrogant Master of Midnight. "Dismissed, all of you."

CHAPTER 6

ERIC CHATTERED ALL THE WAY down the hall. "This whole building is pretty much a square surrounding a central court-yard. We're in the northern wing now. There are a couple of shape-shifters housed here, but mostly it's sitting rooms. There's a seam-stress, and her office is at the end of the hall, right there." He pointed, and then led them through a dark oak door. "This is where most people sleep." Turquoise noted his avoidance of the word "slaves," though that was obviously who he was talking about.

The décor in this wing was just as elegant as Jaguar's sitting room, if not quite as dark.

The oaken panel and chair rail continued from the north wing, but the floors here were polished wood, and the walls textured, pale honey-beige. Sponge painted? Turquoise wondered, amused by the thought of a vampire sponge painting a wall. Though of course, human slaves would have done all the work. Lamps set in the ceiling provided a soft glow.

"Who did the painting?" Ravyn asked, apparently as curious as Turquoise.

"I did," Eric replied proudly. "It was white before. There aren't any windows in Midnight, so I thought something warmer would be better for the sanity of us humans. That's my room," he added, pointing to the first room in the hall. "And here is where you two will be staying."

The room was simple—two stacked beds, currently unmade, sliding doors Turquoise assumed led to a closet, and an empty table. A second door was set in the side of the room.

"There are sheets folded in the top of the closet," Eric said. "Bathroom is through that door; you share it with Lexi and Katie, who are your neighbors. Katie is the woman to talk to about clothing, toiletries, and stuff like that. Lexi . . . she doesn't say much, but she works with Katie. They both usually sleep until about midnight, but after that you'll find them either in their room or in their workspace in the northern wing. Anything else you need?"

Turquoise did have one gnawing question. "How old are you?" Jaguar seemed to trust this boy, and Eric certainly seemed to be in charge of the humans when Jaguar was not.

Eric seemed startled by the question. "Fourteen. I think. Yeah, fourteen." After a moment, he seemed to understand what she was really asking. "I've been here since I was eleven."

Turquoise felt her stomach churn.

"It's not that bad," he said softly. "And honestly, I've got nowhere else to go."

She didn't want to hear this. This boy was her brother's age—the age her brother would have been, her mind forced her to remember. He was what Tommy might have become, if he had lived.

Eric must have translated Turquoise's distressed expression as skepticism, for he continued, "Jaguar found me with the vamps that had killed my parents. He bought me; saved my life." He shrugged. "He trusts me. And I can run this place cold." With a half-smile that seemed forced, he added, "I'm actually one of the lucky ones. Some of the people here with different owners, they don't even know their own names anymore."

Turquoise understood, and did not want to know more. She had seen the human dogs Lord Daryl surrounded himself with. Only through pure luck and dumb stubbornness had she avoided becoming one of them.

Ravyn flopped down to sit on the lower bed, asking, "How many humans are in here?"

"Eighteen in the building," Eric answered promptly. "That's including you two and myself. Two cooks. We could use one more; can either of you cook?" he interrupted himself.

Ravyn nodded. "I can cook."

Eric smiled, and continued, "Great. Besides them, of course there's Katie and Lexi. Two more people work in the infirmary in the south wing. I'll show you there later. That's it."

"That's nine," Turquoise stated.

Eric gave her a look, and then his eyes fell. "The vampires need to eat, you know." The message was clear. "A few vamps live here permanently, and other vampires come and go. Most of them aren't too threatening, but you should be careful. They've been starting to grumble that Jaguar won't let them treat us like they want. Jeshickah showed up about a week ago, bringing her own pair of . . . pets," Eric finished, voice apologetic at the last word. "She's staying in the first room in the west wing, and she doesn't care what Jaguar says she can or can't do. Be careful around her. If she hits you, don't get up. She's less likely to hit you again if you stay down." With that less than cheerful advice imparted, Eric glanced around the room, double-checking to make sure he had not left anything out. "That should be it," he finally decided. "Get some rest; I've got some stuff to do, but I'll be back about midnight to show you the south wing. Oh," he added, "meals are served at sunrise, sunset, and midnight. There aren't enough people awake at noon to make it worthwhile to cook. Nothing fancy is made, but if you want something special, you can feel free to ask. Generally, sunset is breakfast food and the other two are dinner."

"Thanks."

Eric disappeared out the door.

"Should we ditch and explore?" Ravyn suggested languidly.

"We need to talk first," Turquoise responded.

"I suppose." Ravyn yawned. "This looks like an easy job. Get a knife. Put it in the bloodsucker. You can take Jeshickah and I'll get Jaguar, or the other way around, if you'd prefer."

"The assignment was to get rid of Jeshickah," Turquoise reminded her, "not Jaguar."

"Jaguar's the one running things right now," Ravyn pointed out. "We take down Jeshickah, you don't think he's going to object?"

Turquoise shook her head. "Let's avoid picking random targets until we know what's up, okay?"

Ravyn shrugged dismissively, not agreeing. "Once the job's done, suppose I can steal her car?" the hunter asked. "Lamborghini

Diablo . . . that thing's worth three hundred thousand easy, half mil maybe."

"Could we stick to the problem at hand?" Turquoise interrupted.

Ravyn gave her a look as if Turquoise were mad. "It's a nice car. Besides, it'd be fun to figure out. I hear they're almost impossible to steal. I prefer the black, but all things considered—"

"Ravyn." Turquoise's patience was at an end.

Ravyn glared back. "You are no fun."

Turquoise debated strangling her detested partner, but elected to find sheets and make the top bed—Ravyn was still sitting on the bottom one—instead.

Ravyn finally acceded, standing and following Turquoise's example. The sleepy expression she usually wore was gone. "Let's see if Jeshickah is really planning to run Jaguar through. If she isn't . . . Even unpaid, I wouldn't mind putting a knife in the creature that runs the slave trade." For the first time, Ravyn's voice didn't sound tailored.

"How'd you end up involved with the trade?"

Ravyn shrugged. "Wrong time, wrong place, wrong life. Stumbled across a vamp with a taste for exotics." She said the words emotionlessly, as if she were quoting.

Exotics. It sounded like a sign that should be in a pet store, advertising parrots or rare snakes. Hearing Ravyn apply it to herself was sickening. Knowing that Ravyn's burgundy hair and eyes made the description appropriate was worse.

Still, condolences were out of place. There was no friendship between her and Ravyn, and likely never would be. "How'd you get out?"

Ravyn's smirk returned. "Friends in low places," she explained crisply. "I made a couple deals with vampires who hated Jared to begin with. They might not have stopped Jared from taking a two-by-four to me, but at least they didn't stop me from slamming said beam into his skull before I put a knife in him."

After that, Ravyn lost interest in talking except to ask for the top bed, which Turquoise gave up without much of a fight. She wouldn't sleep well in either place.

CHAPTER 7

"*I can't believe I ... I'm so stupid.*" *She took another large gulp of milk, trying to stop the tears.*

"*No you're not,*" *her father argued. His face still held a look of dazed shock, as it had ever since the police had woken him in his hotel room nearly eight hours ago. "Listen to me, Cathy.*"

She lifted puffy, crying eyes to her father.

"*You're Catherine Miriam Minate,*" *he said, as if that explained everything. "You're proud, and you have every right to be. And no one—no one—can take that away from you unless you let them. You're safe now,*" *he assured her. "You can't let this*

*creep have the satisfaction of hurting you. No one
can make you a victim but yourself."*

*She shook her head, remembering how dumb she
had been. A strange city, a strange hotel, a strange
guy . . . why had she trusted him? Even at home,
she wouldn't have let a stranger get so close, no
matter how nice or cute he seemed.*

*Mr. Minate stood and hugged his daughter close.
She could feel his fatigue and his fear. He knew the
danger was over, but was still near to panic.*

Turquoise had forgotten to consider one fact when planning their trip to Midnight: she was claustrophobic. Not terribly; she wouldn't end up huddled, screaming, in a corner, but she hated to be stuck in one small room.

She alternated between napping and pacing. When she slept, she dreamed, and the dreams were rarely pleasant.

Asleep or awake, vivid memories of Lord Daryl's manor assaulted her.

There had been four floors to the house. The top level had held the kitchens, laundry rooms, and quarters for Lord Daryl's numerous common slaves. Turquoise had not been allowed there, but she had explored it once while Lord Daryl had been away. He had beaten her unconscious when he had returned.

The third floor had held mostly bedrooms—hers, Lord Daryl's, and guest rooms. Lord Daryl's studio had been on that floor, a large room in the northern side of the house. It had been the only room in the house with a window, an almost solid wall of glass, and once or twice a month, when she had been desperate for sunlight, Catherine had crept in there despite Lord Daryl's rules. The glimpse of life beyond her slavery was always worth risking a beating.

The second floor had held an office, a desk with drawers that were always locked, the dining room, and the library. Catherine had spent hours reading history, which was a subject on which Lord Daryl had numerous books. She ate alone. Lord Daryl's slaves, even when serving her meals, were silent. Unless Lord Daryl spoke to her, Catherine heard no voice, no sound at all.

The first floor had been one large, elegant ballroom, complete with grand piano, polished dance floor, and a chandelier Catherine never saw lit. Lord Daryl was possessive and paranoid, and kept her away from the rest of his kind. When he hosted parties, he invariably locked his pet away in the next room, where she would barely hear music and distant voices.

That room, the little sitting room next to the ballroom, had been Catherine's sanctuary. The carpet had been soft and black, and the walls had been burgundy so dark that only direct light would make the red visible. The room held a couch and matching love seat covered with black suede. A small bookshelf in the corner held photos of people Catherine did not know, and books in languages she could not read.

Turquoise wrenched her mind away from her past. She glanced at Ravyn, who was lying on her bed and pondering the stucco ceiling, and rejected as impossible the idea of intelligent conversation. Instead, she dropped to the floor and started doing push-ups. Generally, she ran for four miles and then used weights, but this little boxy room wouldn't allow for that.

She did fifty on her right arm, and was up to thirty-seven on her left when someone knocked on the door.

"It's Eric. May I come in?"

"Go ahead," Ravyn called. She jumped down from her bed, commenting to Turquoise, "I'm tired just from watching you."

"I promised you a tour of the south wing," Eric reminded them. "I thought you might want to eat first," he told Ravyn. "Sound fine?"

"Peachy," Ravyn answered.

Eric seemed unnerved by the bright response, but he did not comment.

He showed them to the kitchens, where the midnight meal was being served. They ate, and Eric introduced Ravyn to the others she would be working with.

Afterward, he briefly showed them the infirmary and the weight room. "Keeps people busy in their down time, and gives them something to do to keep healthy," Eric explained about this last.

"What's through there?" Turquoise asked, pointing to a heavy oaken door in the interior wall that seemed out of place.

"Courtyard. It's off-limits. The door's locked anyway," Eric explained briskly.

If a door is locked, you're not welcome, Jaguar

had said. Instantly, this courtyard interested Turquoise. "What's in there?"

Eric shrugged. "You'll have to ask Jaguar about that. Speaking of," he continued, changing the subject, "if you can find Jaguar sometime before you turn in, ask him if I'm allowed to bring you outside. Probably not, but that's where I really need the most help. Otherwise, you'll either be cleaning or bloodletting, whichever you prefer." The boy's tone made it clear he'd have no respect for her if she took the second choice.

They split up. Ravyn returned to the kitchens to learn the ropes, Eric disappeared into his room, and Turquoise sought out Katie. She gave the woman her measurements, and was rewarded with the necessities of life: three full outfits, as well as a toothbrush, hairbrush, soap, washcloth, and two towels.

Next, Turquoise went looking for Jaguar. If all went well, she'd find him quickly and ask about going outside. That should grant her enough free time to explore. She wanted to see the western wing, and she wanted to get into the courtyard.

There were two locked doors in the northern wing; the shape-shifter rooms, Eric had said. The inside wall was empty—no courtyard door here. Jaguar was not in any of the sitting rooms, though she did have to skirt one room where Jeshickah was arguing with a vampire Turquoise did not recognize. The glimpse she caught as she walked by was of an attractive man of maybe twenty years, with a strong build and elegant features.

His words caught her attention, enough that she paused just past the room. "Are you going to kill him?"

Jeshickah paused to consider the other vampire's question. "Jaguar is trying my patience, but he's too valuable to put down so quickly." She sighed. "I'll give him a few days; maybe he just needs a reminder of his place. If he still hasn't come to heel, I can take Midnight back from him."

"He might fight you on it," the other vampire pointed out. "However it happened, Jaguar has picked up a fair amount of independence since Midnight burned."

"And then who will you back?" The vampiress sounded unconcerned.

"The only person I would rather put a

knife in than Jaguar is you." The comment was made as if the knowledge was well known and unimportant. "But if it comes down to a fair fight, you'll win. Who's the human?"

The change in topic startled Turquoise, and she felt a chill as she realized the question was about her.

"Jaguar's new toy. Girl, come in here."

Turquoise obeyed, knowing delay would be painful; she forced herself to recall all of Nathaniel's suggestions, as her excuses came quickly to her tongue.

"Yes, milady?" Eric had used that title without being hit; hopefully she could do the same.

Ow. Her right knee struck the floor hard as Jeshickah's companion kicked it out from under her, inelegantly but effectively forcing her to kneel.

"She suit your fancy, Gabriel?" Jeshickah asked.

So both of the vampires Nathaniel warned Turquoise about were in the same room, while she was alone and unarmed. Fate had a twisted sense of humor.

But Gabriel just replied, "She's more Jaguar's taste than mine." This was not a fun conversation; Turquoise's fingers ached to be wrapped around a knife. Her leg was starting to go to sleep below the knee. "What are you up to?"

The question was addressed to Turquoise. "I'm sorry for interrupting, sir. I was told to speak to Jaguar, but I don't know where he is." The building wasn't that large; she would have found him eventually. But so long as she was playing the part of a dumb slave, she might as well take advantage of its excuses.

Gabriel looked to Jeshickah. "How long has he had her?"

"A few hours."

Without warning, Gabriel dragged Turquoise to her feet; she had to check her desire to slam an elbow into his gut and wrench her arm out of his bruising grip. "The guard on the western wing will direct you to your master. In the future, I suggest you remember to refer to him as such."

He released her. Turquoise resisted both the urge to rub the new bruise on her arm, and the desire to turn about and slug him in the jaw. She left their presence quickly, trying to rid herself of the creeping feeling that she was lucky to still be walking.

A raven shape-shifter blocked the door to the western wing. She shifted into human form as Turquoise approached.

"You have business here?" the girl asked.

She recalled Gabriel's "suggestion" bitterly as she spoke. "I'm looking for Master Jaguar. I'm supposed to—"

Her explanation was cut off as the girl pushed open the door. "Jaguar's study is the third door on the right. If he's not there, you can wait."

Excellent. Apparently, Jaguar's lax rules extended to his guards, who were allowed to send people into his rooms. Turquoise looked forward to the possibility of snooping.

She knocked lightly, and was disappointed to hear Jaguar's smooth voice call out, "Come in."

As she entered the room, Jaguar pushed away from the desk where he had been working and stretched. "Audra, nice to see you. You want something?"

"I didn't mean to interrupt," she apologized, speaking softly and dropping her gaze. The unfamiliar name did not sound strange to her. Outside Bruja, she changed her name with each assignment. She had no fondness for any particular combination of syllables; Audra was as good as Turquoise or any other.

Jaguar shook his head, looking vaguely amused. "Submissiveness does not become you. Don't worry. I would much rather talk with you than do paperwork." He frowned suddenly. "What happened to your wrist?"

A glance revealed red marks where Gabriel's grip had held her. She flexed the wrist, but it was only bruised, nothing more. "One of your guests corrected my misuse of your name," she answered. "It was my mistake."

"I take it your old master wasn't overly fond of titles?"

Honestly, she answered, "Only his." Lord Daryl had not expected her to speak of others of his kind at all. Referring to another vampire as "master" or "milord" in front of Lord Daryl would get her beaten, as if she was acknowledging ownership by another as opposed to him.

Jaguar shook his head. "Please, sit down." He motioned to one of the free chairs as he collapsed back into his own. Turquoise took a seat, though she could not begin to relax as easily as Jaguar did. "Did you come to keep me company, or do you have a question?"

"I spoke to Eric about getting an assignment," she explained, grateful to change the subject. "He wanted me to ask you if I could work outside, since he needs the most help there."

Jaguar paused, and his gaze flickered down her form. "Jeshickah knows you aren't broken. She'll feel the need to correct that error much more quickly if you're working outside. You don't want to encourage her to do that," he recommended. "What other jobs does Eric have?"

"He said cleaning or bleeding."

"Neither of which sounds very fun for you," Jaguar offered.

Turquoise did not argue with him, even though he was more than half wrong. There were humans who chased after vampires all their lives, addicted to the sweet, intoxicating rush of having their blood drawn. It could be very pleasant, if the vampire wanted it to be.

Perhaps that was why it frightened some hunters so much. It took effort to live, to fight for one's life and one's pride. It was too tempting to simply relax and let the blood flow. Too tempting to let yourself slip up in a fight.

Turquoise shook the thoughts from her mind. She had no desire to die, and she certainly had no desire to become some vampire's pet bleeder. She only had to look at the scars on her arms to remind her why.

Like all hunters, she hated putting herself in the prey's position, but unlike most, she did not mind letting a little blood if doing so was an occupational necessity. A bleeder in Midnight would be closer to the vampires than any other human.

"I was a bleeder before Nathaniel bought me," Turquoise explained, modifying the truth as necessary. Lord Daryl had taken her blood occasionally, but he had owned a score of other slaves for such practical matters. She had been more like a lapdog in his manor, ornamental but essentially ineffective.

Jaguar looked surprised. "I wouldn't have expected that."

Turquoise reminded herself that he was a professional, and decided to keep the lies to a minimum. "My first master wasn't much in the way of a trainer, but he did teach me not to fight his orders. After that . . ." She shrugged. "It isn't unpleasant, and it's a lot better than some of the alternatives." Turquoise had seen slaves whose sole purpose was as beating posts to their masters' rage. She knew many who would argue, but she would rather feel teeth at her throat than a fist in her gut any day.

"If you want into that group, go ahead," Jaguar answered, either taking Turquoise's story for the truth or not caring about the lie. "Most of them take the sunrise meal for supper, sleep most of the day, and do as they want at night. Your only other chore is to stay healthy." He continued, "Several of my kind already reside in Midnight, and Jeshickah and Gabriel have both been threatening to move in. Theron doesn't like titles—he generally doesn't want to be addressed by humans at all, so that shouldn't be a problem—but any of the others will hit you if you forget one. If you run across Daryl, tread lightly; his temper is unpredictable." Turquoise was very proud of herself—she kept breathing, kept standing, and kept her expression the same, even hearing that name. "Avoid Gabriel unless you're fond of pain. You aren't, correct?" he asked worriedly.

She rubbed absently at her wrist as she shook her head. "I never have been."

"There are a few others who come and go, so don't be surprised if one of them pulls you aside. I'll tell the guards on the west wing not to challenge you." Jaguar paused, and she could see indecision on his face before he said, "You can go if you want to."

It was not a command, and she wondered why he was offering the permission. He had already made it clear that she could speak freely, and she assumed asking to leave was within the realm of what she could say.

Absently, she brushed back some of the hair from her face, and she saw as Jaguar's eyes followed how the long strands slid across her throat. Though his dark skin did not show pallor as clearly as Lord Daryl's had, Turquoise could tell Jaguar had not fed yet, and she recognized the hungry look in his black eyes.

Testing, she stood, the movement appearing reluctant. "I'll leave you to your work if you'd like."

He answered the way she had expected him to. Not raising his gaze from her throat, he said, "Come here." Though the words were an order, the tone left room for argument.

For a moment, Turquoise almost felt guilty. She was intentionally manipulating him. A feeding vampire is an easy target; most of them completely lost sense of their surroundings as they drew blood. Jaguar did not even try to catch her mind as his lips fell to her throat. If she had been armed, it would have been revoltingly easy to kill him.

CHAPTER 8

JAGUAR RELEASED TURQUOISE reluctantly, holding her wrists until he was sure she could stand on her own. She took a deep breath and leaned back against a wall. He had taken a little more than she would have lost in a hospital blood donation, but it was enough to make her light-headed.

The sound of a throat being cleared in the doorway brought her back to her senses. When she saw who stood there, an instant of frozen panic shoved the fuzziness aside.

Lord Daryl. He wore his customary steel-toed boots; just seeing them made Turquoise's ribs ache in memory. She knew his charcoal gray pants would be dry clean only, as would the blue silk shirt. His hair reflected any color around him like a raven's feathers, and just now it appeared black with blue highlights.

His features looked sculpted from ivory, with just a faint flush—he had fed tonight, but not recently.

And he was beautiful. Why were vampires always beautiful?

In her years as a hunter, she had looked for answers to this. She knew many of them had been changed because their beauty attracted attention. She knew that the vampiric blood erased all the little human flaws, smoothed the skin, firmed the muscle, and in general perfected their form. But knowing intellectually was not the same as seeing.

Beautiful like the Devil, and twice as frightening. Turquoise's heart was suddenly pounding so hard she could feel it against her temples; she knew Jaguar and Lord Daryl both would be able to hear it, but she could not focus enough to slow it. Two years of Bruja training might as well never have occurred.

"What do you want, Daryl?" Jaguar

snapped. Clearly, he did not like his guest. He held Turquoise against himself, either protectively or possessively. Turquoise liked to think it was the first. But Jaguar's protection had its dangers, too. Lord Daryl had always been jealous.

"New acquisition?" Lord Daryl bit out, his gaze falling on Turquoise with instant recognition before it rose to meet Jaguar's in blatant hatred.

"A gift from Jeshickah. What do you want?" Jaguar repeated, his feelings for Daryl mirroring Daryl's for him.

"Has Jeshickah decided whether she is going to stay?" Lord Daryl responded, apparently in no hurry to get to the point.

Jaguar shook his head. "She hasn't told me her plans. If you've got nothing better to do than chat, Daryl, I must ask you to leave. I have work." Daryl started to argue, but did not manage to get a word out before Jaguar added, "Dismissed, Daryl," in a voice so cold it made gooseflesh rise on Turquoise's arms.

Lord Daryl stalked out, fury written in every movement.

"You can just order him around like that?"

Turquoise asked, before she could bite her tongue to stop herself.

"Supposedly, everyone in this building is under my command."

"Why supposedly?"

"There are always exceptions," Jaguar answered dryly.

Jeshickah, Turquoise guessed. And maybe Gabriel.

"Go find something to entertain yourself with, Audra," Jaguar sighed. "I should speak to Jeshickah before Daryl goes whining to her."

Jaguar preceded her into the hallway, which Turquoise entered only with great trepidation. Lord Daryl had barely acknowledged her in Jaguar's presence, but he had recognized her. If he caught her alone she imagined no leniency.

Turquoise halted in the hallway and watched Jaguar leave, leaning back against the wall as if a bit faint, until she could focus and plan her next move.

Lord Daryl was an unexpected danger she would have to cope with. She had her own agenda, to accomplish with or without him in the way.

Right now, she wanted to see the court-yard. She could check the door to the south wing, but she imagined it would be inaccessi-ble at this time, as too many people would be within sight. She would never be able to pick the lock and get inside without being seen.

As she stepped into the hallway on her way to the south wing, Turquoise bit back a curse. Ravyn. Whatever she was doing here, it wasn't in line with their plan to lay low un-til they understood what was going on.

Ravyn didn't seem to be in trouble yet, but she looked pretty near. Gabriel was leaning back against the wall, arms crossed over his chest, and regarding Ravyn with skepticism as she spoke.

Huffily, Ravyn turned away and started toward the south wing; her vampiric com-panion grabbed her arm, pulling her back. Turquoise started to approach, but Ravyn caught her eye and shook her head minutely. She did not look distressed, so Turquoise would let her handle this on her own.

Turquoise returned to her room and paced, waiting for Ravyn. Her energy was ferocious behind the docile front she had to display; she wanted to fight something. She was anxious to complete their mission and leave; she was doubly anxious to know what trouble Ravyn had gotten them into.

Jeshickah couldn't be that difficult a target. Jaguar detested her so Turquoise doubted he would protect her. All Turquoise needed was a knife and a moment of opportunity.

Of course, if she misjudged and Jaguar did get in the way, he would probably have to go, too.

Finally the door opened, and Ravyn sauntered in. The girl looked a bit pale, tired, but pleased as punch.

"What was that?" Turquoise immediately snapped.

Ravyn just stretched, yawned, and without bothering with pajamas climbed up to her bed. "It's almost sunrise, Turquoise. Get some sleep."

Sleep? Strangling Ravyn seemed once again like a very good idea.

"Ravyn—"

"I am tired," Ravyn responded. "And incidentally, I have a plan. Let me sleep, and I'll tell it to you. Later." She pulled the pillow over her head.

Damn that girl.

Sunrise. Most of the vamps would be bedding down to sleep. They weren't comatose under the sun, but a sleeping vampire was still an easier target than a fully conscious one. Sunrise would have been a perfect time to execute whatever Ravyn's plan was.

Turquoise stalked out of the room. The kitchen was full of people eating dinner. She joined them, and lingered until the kitchen closed, at which point most people retreated to their rooms to sleep.

She spent an hour in the exercise room, and then took a quick shower and changed, by which time it was late morning and the wing was almost empty. She remembered Eric mentioning that not enough people were awake to make a noontime meal worthwhile, so midday seemed to be the best time to make an attempt at the courtyard.

Turquoise had snatched a large safety pin and a pen from Katie's office earlier. Unbending the pin and pulling the shirt clip from the pen provided a low-tech but workable pick set, which she quickly employed on the courtyard door.

The lock wasn't particularly complicated, about as sophisticated as most house locks. Turquoise's tools were less than wonderful, but she had practiced this art a great deal, and within three minutes she felt the telltale click of success.

CHAPTER 9

THE COURTYARD WAS STUNNING.

The area was surrounded by the walls of Midnight, their natural stone texture enhanced with crawling ivy, and the ground beneath her feet was soft with thick green moss, dotted with smooth gray stones that rose in tempting seats. Low-growing trees decorated the ground, young willows and Japanese maples that bowed gracefully to their visitor. Slender irises grew from the edge of a small pool, their blooms past but their green leaves rising regally from their mossy bank.

I can see why someone would want to protect a

place such as this. However, she could not see why Jaguar—a trainer, a slave trader, and a vampire—would care for the beauty of irises and ivy, no matter how kind a master he seemed.

She entered the courtyard with careful but quick steps, keeping her eyes open for anyone else that might be here. Jaguar was probably asleep at this hour, but she did not know if any humans or shape-shifters had permission to be inside these walls.

She was nearly at the center of the courtyard when a rustling of leaves caused her to turn, her excuses already on her lips.

"I was just . . ." The words died, useless.

The animal stalked silently from the grove of willows, its dark-amber eyes regarding her carefully.

Turquoise was no expert on felines; she simply knew this one was big. The creature was probably longer than she was tall. It stretched lazily and she saw extended claws press into the moss; one swipe could probably take off her hand. She didn't know enough to identify the breed by its spots, but considering the master of this place, she could make a reasonable guess as to which this one was.

These two, her mind amended, as a second jaguar emerged from the undergrowth. This one was smaller and lighter, and a ragged line of scar tissue marred her muzzle, running to her ear and leaving a trail of pearl where one beautiful golden eye had been destroyed.

Turquoise knew not to panic. These creatures were bigger than most dogs, but they were still animals; she knew better than to run from them.

Instead, she made her voice smooth and calm as she spoke to the female, whose lead the larger jaguar seemed waiting to follow.

"Milady, I didn't mean to invade your courtyard." *One should always address a large, potentially dangerous animal with respect.* She smiled, recalling her father's words on the subject. Of course, he had been speaking about a stray dog at the time—dangerous, but not a jaguar. Her father's mishmash of wisdom and advice formed most of the only good memories she still had.

As she spoke, she edged toward the doorway, careful neither to run nor to turn her back on the jaguar. "I didn't realize this area belonged to anyone but Jaguar, and if you wish, I will certainly leave."

She found her way blocked by the larger jaguar, and had to circle around to avoid him. He stretched in the shade directly in front of the doorway and closed his eyes to return to the nap she had probably interrupted.

"How like a cat," she murmured. "Well, milady, I don't suppose you're going to ask him to move, are you?" The words got no response, but her attempt to edge past the male jaguar did: he drew back his lips, just near enough to a snarl to make her back off.

She could try the other door, but she hesitated to walk into the west wing without knowing what was going on. She would give it another hour or so. With luck, the jaguar would move from the south wing doorway. If not, she would have to try her luck in the vampire's corridor.

To pass time, Turquoise ended up sitting in a patch of sunlight near the pool, working on her story to Jaguar for when he found her here, trying to do nothing that would aggravate the two felines.

The smaller jaguar was the more inquisitive. She joined Turquoise in the sunlight, and shortly proceeded to give her new human companion a cat-bath. Turquoise endured the sandpaper tongue on her back and shoulders, hoping it was a good sign.

Despite her size and capacity for ferocity, the jaguar acted much like any cat: independent, assertive, but at the moment playful. She nuzzled Turquoise in the side until the human stroked a hand down the jaguar's beautiful fur, and then sprawled ungracefully on the ground to chew on a blade of iris.

The larger jaguar had not moved. Turquoise gave up on hoping, and reluctantly approached the west door. She hesitated as she saw the male lift his head. She was near the doorway when it yawned, showing a threatening expanse of teeth, and stood.

The female shouldered her in the backs of the knees and she nearly ended up on the ground again, but she just barely managed to keep her balance.

"Milady, I'm sorry if I'm being rude, but—"

The male jaguar pounced.

With no time to prepare, Turquoise hit the ground on her back; though uninjured by the fall, she braced herself for the feel of the jaguar's teeth snapping her neck.

She peeled open her eyes after a moment to find a very large cat standing over her, its front paws perched on her shoulders.

She might have blinked; she wasn't sure. Either way, it was suddenly Jaguar who was pushing himself to his feet, and offering her a hand to pull her up.

Mutely, she stared at the hand for long seconds.

Within the sunlit boundaries of the courtyard, Jaguar looked as much at home as he had in the exotic confines of Midnight's interior. The sunlight caused his dark hair to come alive with highlights of warm chestnut; his dark skin took on a rich bronze tone.

Recovering quickly, Turquoise stood without his help. "Jaguar—"

All he said was, "Audra, I don't believe I invited you here." His tone was light, almost playful, and she distrusted it instantly.

"You—"

Before she could form the sentence, Jaguar collapsed to his knees next to the other cat, which nuzzled at his shoulder companionably. "Allow me to introduce Shayla, the most beautiful creature living in this building." He paused, tracing the rosettes on Shayla's fur. "Though I doubt Shayla would ever protest being called 'milady.'"

Turquoise's head was still spinning, and the only answer she could form was, "It's what my father used to call our tabby cat when he needed her to do something."

"Shayla is naturally distrustful of most people," Jaguar explained. "And since every enemy I have, she has as well, there is ample reason for her to be wary. You're lucky she took to you so quickly."

"If she hadn't?"

Jaguar's black eyes were unreadable as he turned from Shayla to meet Turquoise's gaze. "You wouldn't be standing here now." He looked away, and when he continued his voice was once again light. "Shayla is an excellent judge of character. Since she deems you worthy, I'll allow you to be here."

"Thank you, milady," Turquoise said with mock formality, addressing Shayla, who did not look up from meticulously cleaning her right forepaw.

Shayla seemed to sense that the atmosphere had mellowed; she chose that moment to pounce, which engaged Jaguar in a round of kittenish play.

Turquoise could not keep herself from laughing. She was watching a vampire *romp*.

Shayla was the one who disengaged first, when Jaguar managed to roll her nearly into the irises. She walked off with her ears perked, her posture saying, "I meant to do that," as she retreated to the trees.

Jaguar remained lounging on the ground. He propped himself up on his elbows to look at Turquoise. "I've been told that I spend too much time in jaguar form, and it affects my behavior. Do you think it might be true?"

"Definitely." He had given her leave to speak as she wished with him, and she sought to explore how far the limits on that freedom stretched. "How long have you known Shayla?"

Jaguar sighed. "I've known her family since her great-grandfather was a kitten.

Shayla was injured by a hunter a few years ago; she lost one eye and nearly lost the other, and she still walks with a slight limp where the bone was set too late. She never would have survived in the jungle, so I brought her here." Jaguar glanced toward Shayla, and Turquoise followed his gaze; in response to the attention, Shayla yawned widely.

"A lot of the older cultures in Central and South America thought jaguars were gods, or messengers of the gods," Jaguar noted absently.

The comment prompted Turquoise to ask, "Your homeland?"

His expression cooled slightly, but he answered, "My mother's." His voice was carefully neutral as he added, "My father was Spanish."

He turned away abruptly, and Turquoise berated herself for asking the question. She would never have asked any other vampire, as they tended to respond violently when questioned about their origins. For a moment, she had almost forgotten what Jaguar was.

Now would be a good time to back off and

let him simmer alone. Vampiric tempers could be volatile, and when set off they could be deadly.

"Jaguar—"

He had assembled his walls again. "It's almost noon, Audra. I'll speak to you later."

She nodded, and watched in mute fascination as he returned to jaguar form and loped back into the grove of trees.

You can stay here as long as you like, he offered belatedly. His voice slid through her mind, unwelcome and threateningly open, almost an apology about his abrupt brush-off.

Turquoise had to fight her instant impulse to throw up walls and keep him out of her mind. While most hunter groups taught how to guard one's mind at least partially against vampires, that was not a skill most humans had, and doing so while Jaguar was already in her mind could only make him suspicious.

As it was, she sensed him pulling back mentally. When he spoke again, his mental voice was fainter, and carried none of the flavor of Jaguar's mind. *Relax, Audra. Enjoy the sunlight.*

She could not tell whether he was sincere or sarcastic.

Shayla tilted her head, curious, as Turquoise sighed heavily and sat on one of the stones. Turquoise regarded the puzzled jaguar tiredly.

"Do you understand him any better than I do?" she found herself asking. Shayla reacted to the words by nuzzling at Turquoise's side.

Why bother to understand Jaguar? The most obvious answer was so she could predict him. An unpredictable opponent is far more dangerous than one whose moves can be guessed ahead of time, and Jaguar would figure prominently in any move Turquoise and Ravyn made against Jeshickah. But nagging at her was the thought that she wanted to understand Jaguar simply because he confused her, and she was not used to being confused.

She was human. She was mortal. She recognized the fact that she was not all knowing. However, in the two years she had spent hunting vampires, she had never met a creature she so completely failed to grasp.

Nathaniel had painted Jaguar as a dangerous, cold foe; she had wanted to plant a knife in the creature upon hearing the mercenary's words. Yet Nathaniel's arrogant Master of Midnight had turned out to seem sincere and open, and she found herself wondering about the contrasts in his character. One moment he was coldly dismissing Lord Daryl, and the next he was affectionately wrestling Shayla. Turquoise did not understand him, and for that reason above any other she did not trust him.

Trust. That was a word she had long ago learned to avoid. The only thing anyone could trust was that everyone else would look out for himself first.

Shayla was trying for Turquoise's attention again; the jaguar was as bad as a kitten wanting a playmate—a very large, deadly kitten, but just as spoiled and restless.

Barely noon, and Turquoise had little she could do for hours. Ravyn had looked exhausted; she would sleep for a while yet. The courtyard, while beautiful, had proved far less interesting than when it had been forbidden. And fortunately, the vampires would mostly be asleep at this time.

She stretched out next to Shayla. The sun felt wonderful on her bare arms. She was pale, having spent most of the past two years following the nocturnal schedule of the creatures she hunted; she could not remember the last time she had simply lazed an afternoon away in the sunlight.

That was exactly what she decided to do. She had not slept much, and combined with the loss of blood, she was tired. She dozed, and then wrestled with Shayla for a bit, then dozed again.

CHAPTER 10

"*First lesson: title,*" he said calmly as Catherine struggled for breath past the pale hand wrapped around her throat. "*You will address me as Lord Daryl.*"

"*Get your hands off me,*" she hissed in return, her voice made hoarse by the difficulty of drawing breath. Lord Daryl backhanded her nonchalantly, and sparks danced in her vision.

"*Say it,*" he ordered, one hand still wrapped around her throat and holding her against the wall.

Instead, she tried to kick him; with reflexes faster than a striking snake he caught her ankle and pulled her off her feet. Her back slammed against the ground hard enough to knock the already scant breath from her lungs, and she choked around a gasp of pain as her head snapped against the polished wooden floor. The world swam; she could not have stood if she had tried.

"Well, Catherine?" he prompted.

"My lord," she growled in response, "you can go to hell."

She started to push herself back to her feet and he kicked her down again, the tip of one steel-toed boot glancing off the side of her ribs hard enough that breathing became instant agony and she wondered if anything was broken. Another couple of those love-taps would probably kill her. But why should he care? He had already killed her family.

The thought gave her the energy to try to stand again despite the ache in her ribs and head, but the attempt was rewarded by another blow.

"Lord Daryl," she whispered, still on the floor, unable to get the breath to speak louder. "You happy now?"

He nodded, those fair, sculpted features betraying nothing past a cool mask of derision. "Almost."

She woke struggling for breath, aching from phantom injuries long healed. That first beating, the first night she had woken in Lord Daryl's manor, had been minor compared to what she had later endured, but it had been the first and that made it the most terrifying in her memory.

A modern American teenager in a white-collar, preppy town, Catherine Minate had never been hit in her life until Lord Daryl had entered the picture. The remembered terror and pain of that first encounter left her with the taste of fear on her tongue, bitter, metallic, and hot.

Shayla had curled up beside her, and the mixture of the midafternoon sun, the jaguar's own heat, and the nightmares had left Turquoise uncomfortably sweltering. Carefully, she moved back into the shaded grove where Jaguar had retreated.

His animal form remained still, curled up on the soft moss, as his voice flitted in her mind. *You okay, Audra?*

She nodded, realized he could not see her, and then formed the thought clearly in her mind: *Fine. Just bad memories.* She doubted Jaguar would be surprised to learn that a slave had a few bad memories, especially a slave who came with such a brutal history written on her skin in scars.

Jaguar startled her by standing and loping toward her. She smiled as he brushed along her side, a soothing but amusingly feline expression of comfort. Again she had a brief touch of his mind, wordless this time, but offering sympathy nonetheless.

He stretched out again next to her, and Shayla lay down at her other side, as if Turquoise was a frightened kitten to be guarded.

Maybe she was. Either way, sleeping with a protecting jaguar on each side successfully chased the memories away from her dreams. She could see why the old cultures had worshipped these creatures: beautiful and proud, they also radiated savage, protective strength.

CHAPTER 11

SHE FELL ASLEEP resting against the beautiful, soft fur of a jaguar; she woke in a very different situation. Sometime while they had both slept, Jaguar had returned to human form. Now he lay on his back, so that Turquoise woke to find herself snuggled against his side, one of his arms casually draped around her waist.

For a moment she paused to admire the beautiful form stretched out beside her: the black silky hair tousled on the ground, the smooth golden-tanned skin that was warm as any human's.

The illusion did not last. Her cheek rested

on his chest, and beneath it there was no heartbeat.

Jaguar woke at the sound of her sigh. She felt his chest rise and fall in a silent breath, and his arm around her waist tightened for a moment in a companionable hug. "Evening."

Evening? Had she slept so long?

Yes. The sun had set, and in the darkness his voice was soft and a little too warm for her liking.

"I'm sorry," she apologized by reflex, as she started to push herself to her feet.

"No need to be," he responded. He did not release her instantly, and she found herself hesitating, trying not to stare into black eyes that at the moment were frighteningly intense. "It's not an unpleasant way to wake up."

Maybe not to him, her mind argued bitterly. He was the owner, not the slave. The choices were his.

He let her go and she stood hastily; Jaguar followed more slowly, but as she stepped out of the grove and into the open starlight he caught her arm.

Her mind kept flashing snippets of memory as she tried to deal with the present.

Lord Daryl had mostly treated her as a disobedient pet. More than once she had fallen asleep—usually still bruised and aching from the last beating—with her head resting on his knee as he worked on some carving, and woken curled in his arms like a child's favorite toy.

"Audra, there's no need to be frightened."

Only when he said it did she realize she *was* frightened, enough that she could feel her heartbeat in her temples and wrists, fast with nervousness. Jaguar and Lord Daryl were nothing alike; she repeated the words in her mind over and over.

The fact that he was a vampire did not scare her; she had hunted enough vampires over two years that they no longer forced terror into her mind.

The fact that she had let her guard down, forgotten even so briefly what Jaguar was, that frightened her. The fact that she actually found him likeable, with a sense of humor and compassion, *that* terrified her.

She might need to kill him; she did not want to start thinking about how human he seemed.

"What are you afraid of?" Jaguar asked,

as she yanked her arm out of his grip. "You had no fear in you until this instant."

She ignored him, picking her way carefully around stones in the darkness and trying to remember which wall the door was on.

"You've bared your throat to me, Audra. You aren't afraid of what I am," he stated. "What else is there?"

She turned back to face him, wishing she could simply sink into the wall she leaned against. "I can't explain."

"Why not?" he asked, and though his voice was gentle she could tell he was not going to let her worm her way out of this easily. "Who is stopping you? I'm your only master here, and I'm not going to hurt you for anything you say."

He stepped toward her, and Turquoise flinched as he planted one hand on the wall to each side of her shoulders. "What are you afraid of?" he asked softly. "Are you afraid I'll recognize that you're pretending to be a slave when you have as much free will as I do? Or are you afraid I'll recognize these . . . ?" With fingertips that barely grazed her skin, he traced the scars on her right arm, finally settling on the ring around her wrist. "And that I'll know whose weapon made this mark?"

Her throat was choked around the knot that must have been her heart, which jumped from her chest at the mere suggestion of Lord Daryl.

"Afraid I'll remember stories I've heard, the ranting complaints of one of my associates? Pretty, but very disobedient, he said. And strong—but of course he would call her strong, since he couldn't seem to tame her. She had a natural resistance; he couldn't get into her thoughts, and didn't know any other way to break her. He called her Catherine."

The silence after he finished speaking seemed to last forever.

She jumped when he reached for her again, but all he did was brush a lock of hair out of her face. Jaguar's proximity was awakening more than her hunter's instincts.

"I'm not going to hurt you," Jaguar repeated. He lowered his lips to her throat, and she relaxed in the familiar position. "What is it that terrifies you not of this . . ." She felt the sharpness of fangs against her throat, not pressing quite hard enough to pierce the skin. ". . . but of this?"

He kissed her.

He kissed slowly, unhurried, as if he could stay all day and not miss a beat. At the same time he was demanding, deepening the kiss before she knew what was going on. Gentle he was not, but the aggressive edge of his kisses was like the sweet rush of adrenaline so dear to a fighter.

Of course, he had a few hundred years of practice, and Turquoise had very little to compare him to—human boyfriends, mostly, and all of those a long time ago. And Lord Daryl.

The last thought made her jump. Jaguar's kiss had none of the violence of Lord Daryl's, but the undertone of possessive dominance was the same, and that made Turquoise recoil the instant she recognized it. She pulled back, slamming her back against the stone wall as she pushed Jaguar away.

"Audra—"

"Jaguar, let go of me."

He hesitated. "Audra—" he began again, and again she interrupted, "Let go of me."

He released her so suddenly she had to bite back a gasp. "I'm sorry."

Turquoise saw the newcomer enter the courtyard before Jaguar did. The vampiress glanced at Turquoise for a brief moment before turning her gaze to Jaguar. She caught him by the shoulders and whispered, "How touching, kitten. It seems you've made a new friend."

Jaguar spun around in a movement too fast for Turquoise's human eyes to follow, recoiling from the vampiress behind him. "Jeshickah." The name fell off his lips as a mixture of greeting and fear.

"Are you enjoying your new pet, little cat?" Jeshickah purred, inclining her head toward Turquoise. Turquoise's hand itched to reach for a knife—if only she had one— the instant those black eyes fell on her.

At the same time, Turquoise heard Jaguar's silent voice. *Kneel.* She cringed at the invasive feel of his command in her head. Jaguar's expression did not change, but his voice was desperate as he added quickly, *Don't fight me now, Audra. Not unless you want her to hurt you.*

The sensation was like sandpaper scraping down her throat as she swallowed her pride and went down to one knee, lowering her gaze so "Mistress" Jeshickah would not see the blatant hatred there. She had been prepared for moments of subservience, but that didn't make her enjoy them.

To Jeshickah's question, Jaguar answered aloud, "Audra has been keeping me entertained."

"She's not very well trained," Jeshickah observed.

Jaguar shrugged. "She's adequate, and I don't have time to work with her."

"Adequate?" Jeshickah's voice sounded amused.

"Do you need something?" Turquoise marveled at how perfectly cool his voice was, after he had been so obviously frightened by her sudden arrival. "You aren't supposed to be here."

"Do I need your permission to enter?" Jeshickah's voice had picked up a dangerous tone, but it was light again when she added, "Besides, I would have hated to miss such a touching little scene with the girl."

Turquoise wondered how much Jeshickah had seen. She also wanted to know when she could stand up; her neck was getting a crick in it.

"As for what I *need*," Jeshickah continued, "we were supposed to have a meeting several hours ago that you neglected to attend."

"I told you I had other obligations," Jaguar answered. Of course, the fact that he was blatantly lying showed his disregard. He had done nothing all day, unless Turquoise had slept through it.

Jeshickah's voice carried a threat. "And I told you to cancel them." Turquoise could only see Jeshickah's feet as she strode forward, until she and Jaguar were nearly touching. "I've been amused so far by your toy replication of my Midnight, and because of that I have allowed you to rule, but I am not amused by what I see now. I am most disappointed with what *you* seem to have become."

"Then go away," Jaguar suggested tiredly. "I've no desire to turn this place into what you made of the last one."

He stumbled back as she shoved on his shoulders. "Don't forget, cat, everything you own is mine. Even the blood that runs in your veins is what I have given you. If I say I want your slaves washing the floors with their tongues, you will make it so. And if I say I want her broken," Jeshickah finished softly, "you will do it."

"I will not," Jaguar responded, his voice just as soft, just as poisoned by anger. "The humans in Midnight are exactly as I wish them to be. Audra is exactly what I wish her to be. Understand?"

The air grew taut with Jeshickah's rage, and this time she slammed Jaguar up against the stone wall hard enough that Turquoise flinched, glad she had not refused to kneel.

"I understand that you think you aren't a trainer any more," Jeshickah spat. "I understand that you think yourself to be in charge here. And I understand that you are a pathetic beast who thinks no one remembers who he used to be."

"Get out of my courtyard."

Again Jeshickah bristled; pale fingers wrapped around Jaguar's throat, holding him against the wall. "You can impress the others, but not me. You were a slave to me, Jaguar. I've seen you bleed. I've seen you cower. I've seen you beg." She pulled him away from the wall just long enough to throw him against it again. "All the power you have now, all the power you use to rule this Midnight—I gave it to you. Displease me, and I will take everything you have and break you over my knee. Do you understand?"

Jaguar stayed against the wall, his eyes lowered, for a moment of painful silence before he finally raised his gaze and, with a voice dangerous as black ice, answered, "Yes. Now get out of my courtyard."

"For the moment." Jeshickah disappeared, and Jaguar slumped back against the wall suddenly enough that Turquoise worried that he really was hurt. She started to move toward him, but the lingering reminders of the moments before Jeshickah had appeared—her still racing heart and the light ache in her head—made her hesitate.

The indecision was solved when Jaguar pushed himself back to his feet. He glanced at Turquoise, and then turned away. "Go get something to eat, Audra."

"Jaguar—"

"Out, Audra." His voice was hard with the order. Turquoise hesitated one heartbeat, worrying about the emotional exhaustion she could see in Jaguar's gaze, before hastening to obey.

CHAPTER 12

"DAMN YOU, TURQUOISE," Ravyn growled when Turquoise slipped into the kitchen looking for her. "You disappeared all day, and then you weren't at the sunset meal—"

"Calm down, Ravyn," Turquoise interrupted. "You don't need to worry about me. I can take care of myself. And keep your voice down, unless you want someone to run tell Jaguar two of his slaves are arguing in his kitchen."

Ravyn looked appropriately chastised for perhaps a quarter of a second. Then Turquoise noticed the bruise blossoming on the left side of the burgundy hunter's face, mostly hidden by her long hair. "What happened to you?"

Ravyn's hand flew to the bruise on her cheek. "Our favorite queen leech thought I was a bit cheeky. If she hadn't had another two vamps within arm's length, she would be dead now."

"You armed?" Ravyn didn't look like she was wearing a knife, but Turquoise knew there were many ways to conceal a weapon.

Ravyn's gaze flit briefly to the doorway to double check that they were alone, and then she responded, "The vampire you saw me with was Gabriel Donovan. He is one of the only people here who isn't terrified of Jeshickah. He deduced our reasons for being here, and donated a pair of knives to our cause."

"Out of the kindness of his undead heart, I'm sure." From the pieces of conversation she had heard, Turquoise wasn't surprised that Gabriel was willing to help kill Jeshickah. She was only wary of why he would help a pair of slaves do it. "What's between you and this vamp?" Turquoise pressed, remembering Ravyn's reaction every time Gabriel's name had been mentioned.

"I've worked with him in the past," Ravyn answered vaguely. "He knows I'm a hunter, but my profession has been beneficial to him before, so he won't be a threat. He's been helpful enough that I'll forgive him for never informing me of his connection to this trade." Returning to the subject at hand, she continued, "You'll find your blade beneath the pillow in your room. Once you get it, I say we make this a race: whoever brings down the target first gets Ms. Red's bonus. You game?"

Turquoise found herself answering Ravyn's bluster in kind. Meeting Ravyn's eye with a level gaze, she challenged, "How about the loser forfeits the title?" Turquoise wouldn't be able to beat Ravyn with a whip, though Ravyn probably didn't know that. She also knew where Jeshickah slept, and as a bleeder she could easily put herself in the vampiress's path.

Ravyn hesitated; she did not want to admit uncertainty in her skills by declining the bet, but she did not want to risk her title by accepting.

The burgundy hunter's intense expression suddenly disappeared, changing to one of modest boredom, as her gaze shifted past

Turquoise. "Eric, hey," she greeted. "The meal's over, but if you're hungry I can dig something out of the fridge."

"I was looking for Audra, but thanks," the boy responded, oblivious to the conversation he had just interrupted. "You have a chance to talk to Jaguar?" he asked Turquoise.

Her last conversation with Eric seemed a very long time ago now, but she dredged it up in her memory and answered, "I'm not allowed outside."

Eric frowned in annoyance. "That's a pain." He turned, sensing the vampire behind him before anyone else did.

Turquoise looked up and recognized the vampire; her mind spun and stalled instantly.

Ravyn glanced at Turquoise and seemed to see the other hunter faltering. With a superb imitation of humility, she asked, "Can I help you, milord?"

Lord Daryl barely paused to look at Ravyn before answering, "You're dismissed." Ravyn exited swiftly, her eyes never leaving the vampire. She paused in the doorway and glanced at Turquoise, who nodded minutely, before disappearing into the hall.

"Eric, you have work to do," Lord Daryl added.

Eric looked at Turquoise for a moment, silent apology clear in his features, but he did not argue with the vampire. With him gone, the room was cleared but for Turquoise and Lord Daryl.

Black, unreadable eyes watched Turquoise as she took in the smallest details of his appearance, remembering vividly how those slender artist's hands could deliver a beating so severe she had begged forgiveness for whatever imagined or real transgression had set it off. Remembering the sharpness of fang in her throat, the seductive pull of his mind as he drew her blood. And of course, remembering the instant pain of his whip turned on her once in a fit of fury.

"Lord Daryl." Her voice was so soft even she could hardly hear it.

"Catherine, how nice to find you here," he greeted, and his tone was polite with an undercurrent of anger, a tone she would have stepped back from had she had anywhere to go. "Imagine my surprise when I saw you with Jaguar earlier." Without warning, he backhanded her hard enough to send her reeling. "Where have you been?"

Turquoise grasped for her lies, searching for a story she could tell to this creature, but all of her clever tales slipped from her reach. Catherine was not a vampire hunter. She was just a girl, a girl Lord Daryl had abducted and terrorized, a girl with no guile and no defense.

"Never mind," he snapped when she took too long to respond. "Come here."

"No," she replied instantly, backing away toward the kitchen. His black gaze fixed on her in anger, and he grabbed her arm; Turquoise wrenched out of his grip and took another step back. "Don't touch me." She could not feign sycophancy, not with Lord Daryl. If he had been any other bloodsucker, she could have played the part of subservient slave, but she did not have the strength to kneel to this beast from her past.

She couldn't fight back, either. Rationally, she knew that fighting would make it obvious that she was a hunter. Irrationally, every fighting move she had ever learned had disappeared from her head the instant he had touched her.

"Don't argue with me, Catherine," he warned.

She stopped backing up. "Don't call me that."

"Catherine?" He laughed as he said it. "It's your name, in case you've forgotten."

Laughter was a good sign—it meant that he was not in the mood to injure. Keeping him in that mood, however, was nearly impossible unless she wanted to beg forgiveness for the last two years of her life.

"Audra," she answered instead. "I'm going by Audra now. I haven't been Catherine in years."

"I really don't care," he answered, and this time he grasped her wrist in a grip she could not easily break. "Come here."

"No," she snapped, putting all her weight into an open-handed blow to his face. The heel of her palm hit just below the eye hard enough that it would have broken something if it had contacted with human flesh and bone. Four bands of crimson appeared where her nails raked across his skin.

Lord Daryl hit back harder, a reminder that if she wanted to trade punches, he would win. Black spots danced in front of

Turquoise's eyes, and her back hit against the sharp edge of the counter as she tried to avoid falling.

"I'm leaving, Catherine, and you're coming with me."

"Don't you think you should discuss that with me, Daryl?"

The new voice came from the doorway. It was calm, almost a purr, but laced with threat all the same.

Lord Daryl grimaced, glanced back at Turquoise, and offered reluctantly, "I'll pay you whatever she cost."

"She isn't for sale to you."

"Really?" Lord Daryl asked, voice dangerously level. "Just to me?"

"To anyone," Jaguar admitted, "but you especially. I happen to be fond of her, and it doesn't appear that she wants to go with you."

Turquoise took a step away from Lord Daryl.

"Fond of her, are you?" he whispered, voice low. Jaguar seemed to sense that he had made a mistake; he said nothing, but looked to Turquoise.

"Lord Daryl—"

She didn't get any further before he struck

her across the face hard enough that she stumbled. Before she could even think of defending herself, he had grabbed her by the throat and thrown her against the wall. A gasp of pain came from her throat, along with another attempt at, "Milord, please—"

"And how have you earned his favor, Catherine?" he demanded. "Does the jaguar think you're *his?*" He hit her again, this time sending her to the floor. "You're *mine*. Don't you understand that?"

"Milord, I didn't—"

A sharp kick caught her in the side, once again forcing the air from her lungs.

Damn him to hell and back, why am I groveling?

Yet she was, because she had always done so. "Milord, he didn't mean—"

The crack of a whip caused her to jump, expecting to feel the leather slice her flesh again; instead, Jaguar's whip wrapped around Lord Daryl's throat, drawing blood. Lord Daryl stumbled, and while he was off balance Jaguar untangled the whip. Then he grabbed Lord Daryl's throat and threw the other vampire against the wall as easily as Lord Daryl had thrown Turquoise.

"You have no right," Lord Daryl protested, shoving Jaguar away. Jaguar gave ground, but stood between the vampire and Turquoise.

"Right of ownership. Even your twisted little mind can understand that one. Jeshickah paid for her, and then gave her to me. She is my property." Each word was clipped, spoken coldly, as if he was talking about a pet. Lord Daryl's eyes narrowed.

"She is not *yours*, Jaguar," he growled. "She was mine to begin with, before you ever bought her."

"And it seems you lost her, didn't you?"

"I didn't . . ." Lord Daryl paused, then smiled cruelly, his hand going to the cheek Turquoise had hit and the four quickly healing lines of blood there. "She wounded me. She drew blood, Jaguar. Even if you have ownership, I have claim."

Turquoise painfully turned her head away, knowing what the outcome of this argument would be. Blood claim was one of the vampires' highest laws. The blood she had drawn from Lord Daryl entitled him to do with her as he pleased; no other vampire was allowed to interfere if her once-master wished to beat, maim, or kill her.

She thought Jaguar might sigh, or even curse in frustration, but she expected him to give in. After all, there were some laws that none of their kind argued with, and blood claim was one of them.

She expected him to do anything, except what he did.

Jaguar laughed.

Lord Daryl looked shocked for a moment, before Jaguar began to speak.

"You're foolish enough to call blood claim here?" Turquoise did not understand what he was saying, and from the expression on Lord Daryl's face, he did not either. Jaguar went on, "Don't bother complaining that you were weak enough for a human to injure you, because I don't care. If you want to cower behind those laws, go to New Mayhem and serve the rulers there. Of course, they do have those nasty restrictions against the slave trade, but if you grovel prettily they might not kill you for disobeying." Lord Daryl nodded slowly, though none of the hatred left his eyes.

"Fine," Lord Daryl whispered. "Do what-ever you want with her. Just watch that she doesn't put a knife in you before I can do it." He stalked out of the room.

Jaguar knelt beside Turquoise. He reached toward her and she flinched.

"Are you okay?" he asked, not touching her, afraid of causing further injury.

Cautiously, she tried to stand. Her left eye was swollen from Lord Daryl's first blow, and there was no doubt a lump growing on the back of her head from when she had been tossed against the wall. The left side of her rib cage was bruised, but she did not think anything was broken.

He had given her beatings worse than this one.

"I'll be fine," she whispered, leaning against the wall as she tried to get her bear-ings.

"Normally, one warning is enough for Daryl, but Jeshickah's been favoring him lately, and he thinks that gives him power. If I'd realized how smug he's gotten, I would have intercepted him before he could get to you," Jaguar apologized.

Turquoise shook her head, and then

flinched at the pain the movement caused. "Lord Daryl will try to kill you, if you don't let him have me."

Jaguar sighed in annoyance. "I don't like murdering my own kind, but for Daryl, I would gladly make an exception. He knows it, too."

He tried to offer a hand when she pushed herself away from the wall, but Turquoise avoided it. She was sore, and would feel worse tomorrow after all the bruises and bumps stiffened up, but Lord Daryl had never intentionally given her any permanent injuries. Even the majority of the scars on her arms had been accidental, not part of a beating.

Right now, though, she could not accept help from his kind. She would not let this small injury be a weakness. It was bad enough that she had frozen when fighting him, bad enough that she had lost every defense she had learned in two years the instant he had spoken her old name. She would not let Daryl turn her into weak prey again.

CHAPTER 13

JAGUAR ESCORTED TURQUOISE back to the courtyard, and brought ice from the infirmary for the bruise spreading on her face, as well as some water and some aspirin, all of which she accepted gratefully.

Turquoise forced herself to stretch to avoid the stiffening of her aching muscles. Doing so hurt, but it was better than running into Lord Daryl again when she was too stiff to lift an arm in self-defense.

She was antsy to get the weapon Ravyn had promised her, but Jaguar, while not exactly hovering, refused to leave. He tumbled with Shayla a bit, and then took a break to leaf through some papers.

"Does Midnight own the town it borders?" she asked, trying to kill time as well as to understand.

Jaguar nodded. "Not quite the entire town. Two apartment complexes, most of the stores, and a couple neighborhoods. The local paper is independent, as are the schools and most of the housing."

"Impressive." She meant it. Running Midnight was one thing; slaves were relatively easy to handle. Running a town filled with free-willed people must have been more difficult.

She didn't want to kill him. Turquoise realized that fact quite suddenly. She did not think Jaguar would try to protect Jeshickah, but any vampire might try to destroy two hunters he found in his territory, and if he did, Turquoise would have to kill him.

Deal with that later, she told herself.

When and if the problem arose she could think these thoughts. For the moment, Turquoise needed this time to return her body and mind to fighting condition. She couldn't afford to face Lord Daryl or Jeshickah as unfocused as she was, and she desperately needed to regain control after the last humiliating confrontation.

As Jaguar continued to work, Turquoise ran through a stunted exercise routine, just enough to warm her up. She didn't have the energy to do her normal full set.

She collapsed onto the moss-covered ground, pausing to catch her breath, and then worked on honing her other senses. Humans relied strongly on sight, but a hunter had to be focused in all ways if she was to survive. Hearing and smell could impart much knowledge about the terrain as well as about the enemy. More important still was the animal instinct for predators.

Humans had no natural predators, and so, like smell, they mostly ignored their latent sixth sense. Strong vampires put off an aura that made even dull-witted humans edgy; a more sensitive human would avoid the leech instinctively.

A trained hunter, like Turquoise, could consciously feel a vampire's presence. The ability made it harder to be startled, and it sped up reaction time in a fight.

She could feel Jaguar's presence, faintly, a tingling on the surface of her skin. From the same direction, she could hear the faint rustling of papers, and the soft sound of his breathing.

Breathing? She opened her eyes. Jaguar was paying no attention to her, and so she had an opportunity to observe him. She was startled to realize that he was breathing, regularly, as a human did. While Turquoise had heard them sigh or yawn or express other emotions, she had never known one who had retained this constant human habit. It was a rather endearing detail.

Jaguar seemed to sense Turquoise watching him; he rolled onto his side, for all the world like a cat himself, to look at her. "How are you feeling?"

"A little sore, but I'll be fine," she answered. "Get anything productive done?"

Jaguar shook his head. "I never get anything done. If I work in my room, someone usually shows up to threaten my life or sell something to me. If I work out here, this girl gets restless." He rubbed his hands down Shayla's muzzle affectionately.

Jaguar's voice was reflective as he mused aloud, "In the original Midnight, Jeshickah had an albino leopard that lived in the courtyard. Nekita, she was called."

"I wouldn't think Jeshickah much of a cat person," Turquoise responded. She tried to picture Jeshickah tumbling with her leopard as Jaguar did with Shayla, and failed.

"When Jeshickah got angry, she'd tie people to the trees in the courtyard so Nekita could sharpen her claws. Usually the victims were humans, or occasionally shape-shifters. Sometimes they were other vampires."

Turquoise grimaced. She did not ask—did not want to ask—whether Jaguar had ever been Nekita's target. "I take it that's part of the original Midnight you decided to change?"

He nodded. "Shayla is very gentle. She'll hunt the prey I bring into this place—rabbits mostly, or birds if they land here—and she'll attack if she's frightened, but if given the chance she would rather retreat than give pain. Only humans have it in their nature to torture."

"And vampires?"

"You think vampire blood gives one the desire to hurt another?" Jaguar responded. He shook his head. "A feeding vampire is as natural and simple as a wolf or a lion. It's only when the human mind is in control that any creature has the desire to give pain."

He gazed at Shayla fondly, and Turquoise recognized longing there—longing to be so innocent. She wondered how Jaguar had survived so long. Sentimentality was a deadly flaw in a predator. Even Turquoise could recognize Jaguar's weakness the way a wolf recognizes the stragglers in a herd.

"The more you describe the original Midnight to me, the less I can picture you as one of its fearsome trainers." Before he could speak, she added, "You don't seem like someone who would enjoy living there."

Jaguar looked surprised for a moment. "You mean the type of person who would enjoy power, wealth, luxury, instant obedience, and virtually anything else I ask for?"

"I mean the type of person who would enjoy manipulating another living creature."

"Why not?" Jaguar responded unnervingly. "We all do what we're good at, and manipulation is a skill I learned very early."

Turquoise shook her head. "You're trying to scare me again."

"Maybe," he answered. "Maybe I don't need to try. Maybe I just need to be honest. I refuse to work as a trainer anymore," he stated, "but that doesn't mean I never did, and that is not work any creature can ever forget. The instinct to analyze, manipulate, destroy, and dominate never goes away. Reason and . . . morals can overlap and control instincts, but they can never destroy them."

He shook his head, his gaze distant. His voice was soft as he added, "I don't want to have to break you."

She didn't like the way he phrased that.

"If Jeshickah takes over Midnight, she won't let you stay here as freeblood. Either she'll kill you, or she'll have someone tame you."

"Lord Daryl didn't manage it," Turquoise stated, bravado in her voice.

"Daryl is too soft," Jaguar stated coldly, and this time Turquoise did recoil. Soft? The creature of her nightmares, soft?

Then Jaguar's voice was in her mind.

Daryl decided to act as a trainer because it was profitable, and he liked power. He can't read people very well, and he certainly has no idea how to control them.

Turquoise would not look away, though she wanted to get as far from the vampire in her brain as possible.

A trainer who knew what he was doing . . . For a split second images came to her, vivid and painful; her knees gave out and she fell to the ground, the phantom taste of blood in her mouth. *You're strong, Audra. But you don't know what you're up against.*

He paused.

Would you like me to let you go?

Yes! Her mind was still reeling from the brief taste Jaguar had given her—a taste of what it was like to be in a trainer's cell, one that would keep her awake at nights longing for the more gentle memories of a beating from Lord Daryl.

Think I have somewhere else to go? she answered, as soon as she could gather her thoughts. She would love to go, to get as far away from Midnight as possible, but she had a job here and would not leave until it was finished. Besides, if she ran now she would need to run forever. One was either predator or prey; a person could not be a hunter if she hid from that which she hunted.

"As you wish." She could feel Jaguar leave her mind, like a subtle pressure draining away. "I'm sorry I hurt you. I wanted to make sure you knew what there was for you to fear."

"Thanks," she answered hoarsely, not yet trusting her legs to hold her if she stood. She forced herself to focus on the job. Information was safe, safer than memories, anyway. "Why is Jeshickah so upset about how you're running things here?"

Jaguar sat beside her. "She wants me to rule Midnight like she used to."

"Don't you?"

Jaguar's expression was shocked. "You don't know much about the first Midnight, if you ask that question."

"Then tell me."

Jaguar's expression was distant as he spoke. "The east wing was a row of cells, each of which usually housed a litter." He hesitated with distaste, and then explained. "The humans were bred for beauty and obedience. Eight or nine children were usually born each year, but it was rare for more than four or five to live past the first culling."

Turquoise choked back bile as Jaguar continued.

"The first-generation slaves, the ones brought into Midnight from the outside, were kept in the combined lower cells, or on occasion in individual trainer cells if they had caught someone's attention." He paused, and then gave an example. "Jeshickah's idea of a well-trained slave would make most of Daryl's dogs seem rowdy, and her methods make Daryl himself seem like a humanist."

Audra nodded, remembering the silent slaves Lord Daryl had surrounded himself with. To her eyes, they had been perfectly obedient, eerily so.

"You don't want to know more," Jaguar stated bluntly, and of course he was right. She had not wanted to know as much as he had already told her. "I worked in the original Midnight for almost two hundred years, until it was destroyed."

"Why did you rebuild it?" Turquoise asked quietly.

Jaguar looked surprised. "Someone was going to."

"Why?"

"Why not?" he responded. "Wealth. Power. The vampire who was threatening to rebuild at the time was generally disliked, and an old enemy of mine." His gaze searched her face for a moment as if wondering whether to say something. He continued, "Daryl, to be exact. You know him well enough to understand that it would have been disaster if he had taken control. Jeshickah had disappeared after her Midnight burned, and Gabriel didn't want to lead, so I was the only one with the power to challenge Daryl." He shrugged, but there was pain in the movement.

"Is he really so strong?" Turquoise asked. Though there were crevices in her soul that held a particular horror of him, a panic that appeared when he was near, in her rational mind she knew he was not powerful.

"Physically, no, but he has political power. He was called a trainer in the original Midnight, and even though his methods were often ineffective, that title gave him a following." Jaguar shook his head. "Still, no one would back him against one of Jeshickah's blood. I'm not quite the strongest in my line, but I'm close enough that the people who originally followed her will follow me."

"How . . ." She broke off, unsure that she wanted to know the answer to the question she had been about to ask.

Jaguar looked at her questioningly. "What?"

"How were your methods different from Lord Daryl's?"

He looked away from her, but still answered. "Daryl's line is known for its ability to manipulate the minds of humans, and he depends on that talent. He uses a simple mixture of brute force, physical and mental, to twist his slave's minds into what he wants them to be." There was contempt in his tone as he continued, "It works about half the time. Frequently, he ends up with products too damaged to be of use. Scarring, for instance," he added, his tone apologetic, "is common on Daryl's projects. I knew you were once his the instant I saw your arms."

Turquoise swallowed the lump in her throat, and forced herself to say, "And how did you work?"

"Pain . . . is easy to give." His voice was

remote, and his gaze rested on some distant point. "Daryl doesn't have the patience necessary to bide his time and observe. Every person has her own weaknesses, physical, emotional, spiritual. After a while, finding those weaknesses and pressing against them becomes a habit, almost a game."

Turquoise remembered uneasily how Jaguar had done just that when she had woken that evening and pulled away from him. He had reacted to her fear almost angrily, like a shark that had caught a blood scent but did not want to acknowledge his attraction to it.

When he spoke to her, was he sizing her up, testing her as a possible opponent? He said he did not want to break her. Did that mean he saw her, a human being, and was content with her actions and reactions? Or was she just a slave he happened to be fond of, and which he would wait to tame until she ceased to please him?

Her thoughts were cut off as Jaguar looked up abruptly. He muttered a curse under his breath and then jumped to his feet.

Stay here.

Turquoise ignored the words and followed

Jaguar. She swore at a rock that nearly tripped her, and arrived in the southern wing just in time to hear the crack of Jaguar's whip and a loud string of colorful expletives from Ravyn. Ducking, she narrowly avoided the knife that Jaguar's whip had caught and tossed across the room.

I thought I told you to stay put.

She did not respond to Jaguar, and he did not insist on an answer. They both had more pressing issues to deal with.

Ravyn had her back pressed to the wall; her hair was in disarray, and she stood stiffly, favoring her right leg. Her gaze flickered to Turquoise briefly, and then returned to the two vampires in the room with her.

Jeshickah was leaning against a table; despite a slit in the side of her shirt, which had probably been made by Ravyn's knife, she looked unfazed. Her gaze was fixed on Jaguar.

Jaguar snapped the whip to disentangle it from Ravyn's wrist; Ravyn hissed in pain, and from the doorway Turquoise could see blood on the burgundy hunter's skin.

"Are you in the practice of letting dangerous pets run about like feral dogs?"

Jeshickah asked acidly, causing Jaguar to stiffen. "Or are you completely out of control of your own property?"

Audra, out. The command was forceful, inviting no disobedience.

However, one does not leave one's allies to get slaughtered, even if those allies are the likes of Ravyn Aniketos.

Audra. The second voice rolled through her mind like honeyed blades, a combination of sweetness and threat. *Aren't you going to obey your master?*

The words loosed a vivid memory, intentionally Turquoise knew.

Catherine, aren't you going to obey your master? *The vampires's voice slipped into Cathy's mind at the same time that Jeshickah said aloud,* "Your pet is rather poorly behaved, Daryl."

Lord Daryl wrapped an arm around the human's waist, and attempted to pull her back against himself, saying, "She's a work in progress."

Cathy slammed a heel down onto the bridge of Lord Daryl's foot and wrenched herself out of his grip, asserting, "I am not your pet."

Lord Daryl was trying to impress this

Jeshickah, whoever she was. Cathy refused to be a good little slave so he could flaunt his power.

She saw amusement in Jeshickah's expression, and then fierce rage in Lord Daryl's, and belatedly realized that making him look like a fool in front of this particular member of his kind had been a really bad idea.

The first blow brought the taste of blood to her mouth. The second was a slug to her gut, and it sent her to the ground, gagging. The third was a kick to her rib cage. Normally, he would stop hurting her once she was down, but normally he wasn't nearly this furious.

The memory was enough to kick the hunter into action.

Turquoise dove, trusting the vampires to be unprepared; she rolled, grabbing the knife Ravyn had lost, and was almost to her feet by the time Jeshickah reacted.

Jaguar shouted, but Turquoise did not turn her attention to him; instead, she tried to keep Jeshickah's backhand from striking her across the side of the face. The blow would have been crippling, had it connected.

Every fighter has an instinctual tendency to defend first, then attack; that tendency has

ended many a hunter's life. Only one ineffective defense means death, but only one effec-
tive attack means victory. If that attack is
fast and hard enough, there is no chance of
losing because an opponent has no chance to
fight back.

Her left shoulder contacted with the vampiress's gut, knocking her off balance. In the
instant before Jeshickah could recover,
Turquoise raised the knife in her right hand.

The crack of a whip echoed dimly in the
back of her mind.

Then blackness.

CHAPTER 14

LORD DARYL SHOVED HER AWAY, *toward Nathaniel. She couldn't get up again. Everything was bleeding, bruised, throbbing. She barely heard her master's voice, shaking with pain and fury, order Nathaniel, "Get her out of here."*

"And where should I take her?" Nathaniel responded, barely glancing at the human who had collapsed at his feet.

Lord Daryl spat another curse, and then disappeared, leaving Turquoise alone with the other vampire. Nathaniel hooked an arm around her waist to help her stand, and wrapped a cloth around her bleeding wrist as he told her, "You have no idea how many people have wanted to do what you just tried.

For that alone I'm willing to help you. Can you walk?"

He set her on her feet, and his answer came immediately; her legs buckled, and the world slid into gray oblivion.

Turquoise forced her eyes open, dragging herself out of an unwanted sleep. Despite the agony of the memory, there was a faint smile on her lips as she remembered the feel of the knife slicing open her master's skin. If only that first, painful attempt had worked.

The smile disappeared as she sat up and became aware of the chain connecting her left wrist to the wall. The back of her head pounded where Jaguar's whip had hit her. She was chained on one side of a large cell; Ravyn was similarly bound a few feet away.

Arguing voices made her headache worse.

"Hunters," Jeshickah spat, pacing angrily, and Turquoise winced at the sharp sound the vampire's boots made as their heels contacted with the cold stone floor. "How could you be so stupid?"

Jaguar did not rise to the bait. "If memory serves, you used to collect hunters. And incidentally, you were the one who bought them."

Jeshickah tossed her mane of black hair in a dismissive gesture. "There is a difference between keeping a well-caged rattlesnake on the shelf to display and letting it slither between your bedcovers," she pointed out acidly.

"I doubt the hunter ever posed any great threat to you."

"Of course not," Jeshickah answered haughtily, "but it's the principle of the thing. You can't allow your pets to go around attacking the guests."

"They were well behaved with me. What exactly did you do to her?" Jaguar leaned back against the wall. He glanced in Turquoise's direction once, but did not acknowledge if he had noticed she was awake.

"Nothing unexpected." With a frosty look at Ravyn's slumped form, Jeshickah added, "Though I suppose your lapdogs don't expect their masters to hit them, do they? Not when you shower them with praises and treats all day long."

Ravyn moaned as she woke, her hands

flying to massage her temples, the chain from the wall to her wrist scratching loudly over the stone floor. She raised a brazen, garnet glare toward the two vampires, who returned it with twin expressions of distaste.

"Either deal with that," Jeshickah drawled lazily, "or give it to me and I will."

"I'll deal with her. I don't prefer your methods," Jaguar answered.

Jeshickah replied glibly, "Oh? And what do you think would be appropriate? A hug and a lollipop?"

Jaguar started to respond, but Jeshickah interrupted him.

"Deal with it, Jaguar," she ordered. "If you don't, I will. I know a few people who would pay dearly for them, after I break them."

"I'll take Catherine back." That voice belonged to Lord Daryl. He had been standing in the corner, so silent that Turquoise hadn't noticed him.

"They're mine," Jaguar argued, barely sparing a glance for Lord Daryl. "I'll deal with the two however I like, and that is not going to involve turning them over to either of you."

Jeshickah's black gaze smoldered. "They

are yours, little cat, but *you* are mine. Blood and body, mind and soul, you belong to me and always will." Jaguar took a step back from her. "You've had long enough with them." Jaguar started to argue, but Jeshickah interrupted him. "You aren't the girl's nursemaid. Daryl's incompetent, but at least he isn't a softhearted baby-sitter."

Lord Daryl's insulted protest was ignored.

Turquoise could see Jaguar thinking quickly, trying to come up with a way to keep her from Jeshickah and Daryl. "Give me three weeks with them," he bargained.

"I don't think you could handle the both of them," Jeshickah argued.

"Let him keep the red-haired one," Lord Daryl suggested. "I want Catherine."

"Did I tell you to speak?" Jeshickah snapped, before turning back to Jaguar. "A few hundred years ago, a couple days would have been more than enough for you."

"She's spent too much time with Daryl; she's built defenses," Jaguar swiftly countered. "Give Ravyn to Gabriel; she's his type."

"One week with Daryl's pet," Jeshickah allowed.

"Two."

"Unnecessary," Jeshickah argued.

"Jeshickah—" Lord Daryl again tried to interject his opinion, only to be cut off as Jeshickah tossed him casually against the far wall. Lord Daryl stayed sulking in the corner.

"One week," Jeshickah repeated. "No special privileges or protection, no silken pillows or puppy treats. I want her licking your boots, or I'll take her from you, train her myself, and have her slit your throat. Understand, kitten?"

Jaguar lowered his gaze for a moment, and then returned it to her face. The moment of submission was brief, but visible all the same. "I understand," he answered, voice tight with barely controlled anger.

"Good." She disappeared, at which point Jaguar swung around and slammed the heel of his palm into the wall. Turquoise winced at the sound of flesh meeting stone, not sure whether the sharp *crack* came from the stones breaking, or Jaguar's hand.

Turquoise had not stood. Instead, she had discreetly worked the safety pin and pen cap out of where she had taped them to the inside of her pants cuff. Her body shielded from view her right wrist as she worked on the lock.

Trying to ignore Lord Daryl, who was glaring at Jaguar but had not yet spoken, Turquoise raised her gaze to Jaguar's.

"What now?" Her voice was calm, and betrayed none of her thoughts. The lock was a tricky one, and doing it one-handed behind her back did not make the job any easier. Once it was open, she had no idea what she would do, but she didn't have many other options.

"Get out, Daryl," Jaguar ordered.

"I think I would like to hear the answer to Catherine's question first," Lord Daryl replied.

Jaguar glared at the other vampire, whose expression instantly shifted to surprise. Turquoise could tell there was some silent communication going on between the two, and she would have given good money to know what it was—especially when Lord Daryl smiled.

"That settled?" Jaguar asked coolly.

Lord Daryl nodded slightly. "Fine."

Focused on their exchange, Turquoise's

concentration broke. The safety pin slipped, and she heard the lock click back into place.

"Would you like me to unlock that?" Jaguar asked, hearing the sound.

"That would make things easier," Ravyn drawled. "While you're at it, would you mind opening the doors and then going out to lunch?"

Lord Daryl's lips twitched again in amusement; Turquoise was beginning to get nervous.

Jaguar smiled wryly. "You," he told Ravyn, "are not my problem anymore." He tossed the keys to Ravyn, who had her lock undone in an instant. She stood, eyeing Jaguar and Lord Daryl warily.

"You're not going to let her out," Lord Daryl argued.

Jaguar ignored him, and continued to speak to Ravyn. "You'll be in the west wing as soon as you go through that door. Gabriel is staying in the second room. I hear you two have a . . . business relationship?"

Ravyn nodded, handing the keys back to Jaguar. "We're very close," she purred. She started to leave, the grace of her exit marred only by a slight stiffness in her walk.

Lord Daryl grabbed Ravyn's arm, and the hunter froze, her gaze flashing to Jaguar. She was obviously sizing up the situation, debating whether to fight Lord Daryl off.

"She isn't yours." Jaguar's voice was cool, the very absence of expression in it a warning.

"She isn't yours, either," Lord Daryl countered.

Jaguar stepped forward, and put a hand on Lord Daryl's wrist above where the vampire was clutching Ravyn's arm. Lord Daryl's grip on Ravyn tightened, and Jaguar's grip on Lord Daryl did the same. Turquoise saw Ravyn's eyes flicking from the faces of the two vampires to the doorway.

"Gabriel will not be pleased if you mark her." Lord Daryl winced as if Jaguar's grip was getting painful.

"She can't just wander around." There was a moment of pause, and then Lord Daryl added, "Let me go."

Turquoise leaned back against the wall, content to watch the vampires engage in their game of male dominance.

She flinched at the sound of bones crunching.

Lord Daryl shouted a curse, flinging Ravyn away, and swung a punch at Jaguar. Ravyn instantly took advantage of her freedom to disappear out the door.

Jaguar grabbed Lord Daryl's wrist before the blow hit and twisted it behind the fair-skinned vampire's back; Turquoise heard the wet snap as tendons in the elbow joint tore. Lord Daryl whimpered, and Jaguar wrapped a hand around his throat.

"Midnight is my property," Jaguar stated, "and so long as you are here, you will obey me. Understand?"

Lord Daryl started to struggle, and Jaguar's grip tightened until Turquoise looked away from the sickening sound of her former master's windpipe collapsing.

"Understand, Daryl?" Jaguar repeated.

Jaguar dropped his captive, and Lord Daryl fell to the ground, his hands at his throat. Turquoise watched, her emotions a mix of distaste and surprise. Here was the creature who had tormented her, terrified her, emitting soft sounds of pain from his crushed throat as it quickly healed. For the first time since the day she had first learned his title, this black-haired creature ceased to be Lord Daryl. He was still stronger than she was, physically, but he was no one's master.

Daryl slid away from Jaguar. He pushed himself up, and coughed a couple times before answering, "Fine." He leaned back against the wall, and rubbed his throat.

"Out, Daryl," Jaguar ordered again. This time Daryl obeyed without hesitation.

CHAPTER 15

"AS FOR YOU ..." He tossed the keys to Turquoise and then sat cross-legged in front of her. "I could not let you kill Jeshickah. The woman has very powerful friends who would have killed you shortly after. I didn't expect that to be a problem when I hired Jillian Red to find me some hunters, but unfortunately I seem to have become quite fond of you, and it would distress me to see you tortured to death." He spoke with a calmness that belied the violence of his fight with Daryl.

Turquoise unlocked her cuff. "You hired her?"

Jaguar nodded. "She's a witch, very powerful and very well informed. I believe she worked with Nathaniel to destroy the original Midnight, so I didn't think she would have any hesitation to help this time."

"I'm confused," she protested. "You worked in the old Midnight, but aren't upset it was destroyed. You founded this Midnight, and are actually trying to ruin it."

"I'm very happy with Midnight as it was two weeks ago. Jeshickah wasn't. Her authority always has been and always will be higher than mine. Either I can let her turn my haven into her own empire again—and she has the power to do it—or I can get rid of her."

Turquoise nodded, contemplating. "How long have you known who Ravyn and I were?"

"I was suspicious the moment I saw you," Jaguar answered. "Nathaniel rarely trades in flesh, and his selling me two strong women, both unbroken, just a few days after I hired Ms. Red . . ." He shrugged. "I wasn't sure until I saw you go for the knife, though. Jillian picked you well. I knew you used to belong to Daryl, and Ravyn's description rang a few bells when I asked around. The more I learned, the more likely it seemed that you two were both exactly what you were pretending to be—two humans who got tangled up in the trade, and were lucky enough not to be broken yet."

"It's the truth," Turquoise answered, with a bit of a smile. "You just neglected to account for the two years after I got out."

"It also didn't occur to me that anyone who had escaped the trade would ever be mad enough to put herself back in," Jaguar pointed out.

Turquoise shrugged. "You're the second person who's called me mad in relation to this job," she commented. "How will you get rid of Jeshickah now? And what do you plan to do with me for the next week?" Unless Jaguar could get rid of Jeshickah before those seven days were up, either Jaguar was dead or Turquoise would once again be a slave ready for breaking. Turquoise would trust no one to put his life above her freedom.

"I have a few ideas for Jeshickah, but none of them are quick," he answered. "As for you . . . I don't know."

Turquoise didn't intend to give Jaguar time to make a decision. She would get out of Midnight today, if he left her alone for more than five seconds. This job had gone bad. If Jaguar had been honest in his warning that killing Jeshickah would bring about deadly retaliation, then Turquoise needed to backtrack and plan again. Confronting Jillian Red and Nathaniel about whether she and Ravyn had been sent on a suicide mission sounded like a good idea.

Getting out shouldn't be too difficult. It would be the easiest thing in the world to scale the courtyard wall and go over the back of the building. The iron fence was high, but she could manage it. Turquoise wasn't worried about Ravyn; the hunter could look out for herself. Whatever Ravyn's relationship was with the vampire to whom she had been sold, Turquoise was more than happy to turn her back on the pair.

She was silent for too long, debating. Jaguar asked casually, "What's Catherine's story? How did she end up in Daryl's care?"

"Doesn't he acquire most people the same way?" Turquoise retorted defensively as she tried to avoid answering.

Jaguar nodded. "He buys most of his slaves from other trainers." He added, "And he doesn't buy anyone who isn't broken. That means he picked you up somewhere else."

"Guess so." She did not feel like sharing her life history today.

"How many people did he kill to get you?"

The words were blunt, and Turquoise knew her shock showed on her face. Most of the scars on Turquoise's arms were from when Daryl had thrown her father through the second-story bay window, and she had almost followed through the broken glass. Before she meant to, she answered, "My mother. My father. My brother." *Tommy*. The thought of her little brother made something in her gut wrench. He would have been fourteen now. "How the hell did you know?"

"I don't know your exact history with Daryl, but I know his methods. He wouldn't have taken a freeblood human without making sure she didn't have a home to return to."

She shrugged. "I wouldn't have had anything, even if they had been alive. How would they ever have understood?"

Jaguar didn't argue with her. "You miss them?"

Turquoise shrugged. "I miss Catherine's old life, sometimes. Her friends, her family. Mostly, the sense of safety she lived with. But I can't go back, no matter how much I would like to." Recklessly, she asked a question that she knew would end the conversation. "What about you? When Jeshickah changed you, did you miss your past?"

Jaguar recoiled as if she had struck him, but he matched her honesty as he told his own brief story. "My mother was a shapeshifter. Midnight's laws didn't allow for shape-shifters to be traded, unless they were first sold into it by their own kind. My father was happy to oblige." He gathered himself quickly, but his voice was still sharp when he answered, "He sold me to Jeshickah for less than the cost of a bottle of whiskey. I could have fought him on it—I was twenty years old, and held almost as much power in the estate as he did—but I was glad to leave." He stood, turning away from Turquoise, each movement slick and angry like a restless, caged beast.

"Why did Jeshickah want you?" Though anxious to leave this fouled job behind, she was genuinely curious about his background.

Jaguar rounded on her, asking, "Why did Daryl want you?"

"Answer for an answer?" she translated. At Jaguar's nod, she explained as succinctly as possible, "My father took me to New York for my eighteenth birthday, to see a musical. We got in late, and my father went to bed, but I stayed in the hotel lobby to people-watch. I was a naïve idiot; when Daryl came up to me, I didn't think past the fact that he was handsome and seemed to be flirting. We were in an open area, surrounded by people. No danger. I never recognized what he was—never even knew vampires existed—until he bit me."

"Daryl's line is weak physically," Jaguar commented, "but if you let one of them in your mind you won't ever think to fight them. Against an unprotected human mind, he wouldn't need to be strong."

Turquoise raised one brow. "Apparently he did need to be." She finished the story quickly. "Or maybe he was just careless. Either way, he didn't manage to catch my mind. I started to fight him, smashed my soda glass against his temple, kicked . . ." She remembered fondly that memory, less fondly the one after. "I caused enough of a scene that he couldn't keep people from noticing, and had to let me go . . . for the moment, anyway."

Jaguar nodded, knowing the gist of the rest, if not the details. Daryl did not kill most of his prey, but he did not like losing one. If Catherine had not fought him, her interaction with the world of vampires might have ended on that night. But thwarted once, Daryl had been twice as determined to claim her.

"Daryl hates you too much to have let you go willingly," Jaguar observed, "and even with his temper, he wouldn't have scarred you unless he planned to kill you. Yet you somehow managed to get out and become a hunter. How?"

"I fought him. I got out. I joined Bruja," Turquoise answered vaguely, her tone adding the words *end of subject*. One of

Nathaniel's conditions for his help had been her silence about his part in her escape. "What about my question?"

"Jeshickah picks her trainers for physical beauty, mental acuity, moral void, and what she calls a trainer instinct—the instinct to watch a person, determine her weaknesses, and destroy her." He paused, and then added, "I had shown a knack for such. It also didn't hurt that Jeshickah had a fondness for shape-shifter blood." He said the words dispassionately, the same way Ravyn had referred to her master's taste for "exotics." Turquoise wondered if she would ever be able to look at her own experience as a slave so unemotionally.

Turquoise had seen how deeply Jeshickah's claws of ownership went. Unless she counted the years before his father had sold him—a very small portion of his long life—Jaguar had never been free.

Physical beauty and mental acuity— Turquoise could still see those descriptions applying to Jaguar. Moral void, she could not. "What changed?" she asked.

"A hundred years without Jeshickah," Jaguar answered. He spoke slowly, choosing his words with care. "There was a slave of mine who survived when Midnight burned. I had owned her since she was four, when I had bought her in one of my many attempts to annoy Jeshickah—she had been born blind, and Jeshickah had been planning to kill her." He smiled a bit at the memory. "She was faultlessly obedient. That was unsurprising; she had been raised a slave in Midnight. Only after Midnight burned did I realize that I had never once struck her. I had never needed to."

He sighed, his expression distant. "Over the years I realized I didn't want to own her; I wanted to know her. I enjoyed her company, especially once she grew brave enough to speak freely with me. She trusted me implicitly, and I was wary of betraying that trust.

"I'd had people fear me, hate me, envy me. . . ." He shook his head. "Trust was new, and it was precious. It took me a long time to figure out how I had managed to earn it."

"And when you did?" Turquoise asked, caught up in the story.

"I realized I didn't think of her as a slave, and that I hadn't treated her like one since

Midnight's walls fell. You can't earn a slave's trust, or loyalty—only her obedience. But blind obedience doesn't make for interesting conversation or companionship; I prefer spending time with a defiant equal more than an obsequious slave." Jaguar shrugged. "I'd be lying if I said I always enjoy the challenge. The relationship between master and slave is clear-cut, easy, and sometimes it's tempting to slip into the familiar role and demand submission from someone who is refusing to give me what I want."

"Such as?" Turquoise pried, thinking of how easily he had ordered Daryl away, and wondering whether that was an example of his giving into temptation, or simply a good decision.

Jaguar laughed a little, shaking off the question. "You don't want to know the answer to that one."

She frowned, wondering if he was laughing at her or at himself.

"We should go outside," Jaguar said. "I need to find Jeshickah before she starts hurting my people, and the courtyard is the only area in this building that's free from Daryl."

He escorted her to the courtyard, his

mood contemplative. Heavy clouds hid stars and moon from sight, and Turquoise welcomed the darkness that matched her mood.

She jumped as Jaguar caught her shoulders, pulling her forward in an impulsive embrace. He kissed the top of her head.

"I know," he said, holding her loosely enough that she knew she could pull away if she tried, "that you are going to disappear as soon as I turn my back."

Turquoise did not argue; there was no point to it.

"That being so, I have one favor to ask." He nodded toward the alcove where he usually napped during the day, and Turquoise's eyes reluctantly made out Eric's form there. The boy was watching them warily, as if thinking he should leave but not wanting to. "Take him with you?"

"What?"

Eric would be a liability. If Turquoise had to protect him, that would make facing anyone she encountered on the way out more difficult. Eric would slow her down. Unless Jaguar was willing to help . . . no. Jaguar would give her the opportunity to leave, but he couldn't afford to help her.

Jaguar all but echoed her thoughts. "In a couple weeks, Jeshickah will be . . . out of the way. Until then, she's going to cause trouble. I doubt she'll kill me." *Isn't that reassuring?* Turquoise thought, as Jaguar continued, "But she won't hesitate to hurt me, or to go through my possessions to do so. She knows I'm fond of you, but you can handle yourself against Jeshickah. Eric . . ." He shook his head. "He's tough, but he's a kid. I can protect him against almost anyone else, but Jeshickah could destroy him, and she will, because she knows I would keep him safe."

What on Earth would Turquoise do with a kid once she got out? Eric had no place in Bruja—he was a victim, not a fighter—but Bruja was all Turquoise knew. Bringing this boy along would play hell with her plans.

But leaving him behind would be leaving him to die.

She nodded sharply.

"After you get out, I recommend laying low until Jeshickah's gone. She'll be raising merry hell."

Turquoise smiled wryly.

He hesitated, and Turquoise could read

fear, desire, longing, and an oversized portion of regret on his face. "I doubt you'll
want to come back to my world, even after
Jeshickah is gone. Would you mind if I came
to visit yours?"

Turquoise swallowed, trying to shove
down the lump of nervousness in her throat.
Jaguar had disrupted her life enough as it
was. Eric was going to mess it up even more.
Continuing her association with the vampire
any longer than necessary was a bad idea.

"I'm planning to disappear for a while,"
she answered. "If I don't want you to find
me, you won't." That was honest, and it
would give her a chance to think.

He accepted the answer. "Best of luck,
Audra."

And then the world shifted, and he was
gone.

CHAPTER 16

THE AIR BARELY CLOSED on the space Jaguar had occupied when Turquoise turned to examine the wall. The natural stones would be perfect for climbing, with plenty of handholds; scaling it would be easy.

Reluctantly, she turned toward Eric. He was fourteen, still a kid no matter what he had seen. He needed a family; instead, he had Midnight. He needed a father; instead, he had Jaguar, who was so tangled in webs of dominance he could hardly help himself.

She was getting sentimental, and that was dangerous. Time to get out of Midnight while she still could.

"Do you want to come with me?" she offered, while the sane part of her mind berated her with every possible insult it could consider.

Eric nodded.

"It's going to be rough," she warned. "I'm no good at taking care of other people." A vision of Tommy assaulted her suddenly, a vision of Daryl striking him down. She tried to shake it off, but it wouldn't disappear.

"I'm okay at taking care of myself," Eric assured her.

Please, don't let me let him get hurt, Turquoise pleaded of whatever powers existed.

"We're going over the back wall. Stay low at the top. Can you climb?" she asked belatedly.

Eric nodded.

Turquoise boosted the boy up, making sure he could find handholds in the rough stone before she followed. They stayed low on the roof to avoid making themselves into silhouettes, and crossed quickly to the back.

The wall here was smooth, and offered no purchase for climbing down. The guard was nowhere to be seen as Turquoise turned and gripped the edge, lowering herself as far as possible before letting go and falling. The impact was jarring, but she knew how to take a fall. She reached up to catch Eric, who mimicked her strategy.

Turquoise's peripheral vision caught movement the instant Eric dropped, a faint blur of color—a cougar. She saw its muscles bunch to pounce.

She twisted awkwardly, pushing Eric behind herself and out of the cougar's way. Off balance, she took the brunt of the creature's initial rush; stars spattered her vision as her back struck the gravel, and she felt claws bite into her skin.

The guard's hesitation was her salvation. Turquoise belonged to Midnight, and the cougar was reluctant to permanently damage her. Turquoise took the moment to get a knee between herself and the cat and shoved full force, sending the guard stumbling a couple feet.

Turquoise was now at a disadvantage. She wasn't sure what the best way to fight a large feline was, but run and hide sounded like her best option. She thought she could make it over the gate before the cougar could follow, if she could delay it long enough for Eric to get out of the way first.

"Eric, over the fence," she ordered.

The cougar moved to intercept the boy, and Turquoise pounced, throwing her entire weight against the cat's side. It snarled, turning on her.

Luckily, the shape-shifter was just trying to contain Turquoise as it waited for its master to appear. Turquoise was grateful for the guard's unwillingness to harm its employer's property, and tumbled at the large cat recklessly, keeping it occupied as Eric scaled the fence.

The hair on the back of Turquoise's neck rose as a familiar aura brushed her senses.

Daryl. She turned and struck in one movement. It's just Daryl. Not Lord, not Master. Just Daryl.

This creature was only another leech, no matter what else he had been to her in the past. He was vulnerable, and she had spent the last two years of her life learning how to make use of that fact. Unfortunately, without a weapon, she still stood about as much chance as a Hawaiian snowman. Still, she would fight rather than submit to this beast.

Her first blow caught Daryl in the solar plexus; it was not as incapacitating a blow on a vampire as it would have been to a human, but it did hurt, and interrupted any attack he had been making. At the same time she knocked out his knee with a side kick, striking just below the joint in a move banned from martial arts competitions because it was crippling to a human.

Crippling for a vampire meant he stumbled. The joint dislocated, and Daryl tumbled with a curse. A dislocated knee, which on a human might never completely heal, would take a vampire two or three minutes to recover from.

Daryl had a low pain tolerance for one of his kind; as she fought, she saw that weakness come into play. He had been startled by her initial attack, and now pain was making him take too long to defend himself.

A fight between a vampire and a human almost always goes one of two ways: either it ends instantly, or the human dies. A vampire is stronger, faster, and can heal more than any human. If a fight lingers, the human will always tire first. Once prepared for a fight, all a vampire needs to do is wait, providing minimal exertion to defend himself.

She had a chance for one more attack while Daryl was bent over, a side kick to his temple. It was a risky move; he could catch her foot and tear it off if he recovered enough to react. However, a broken neck would get him out of her hair long enough for her to get away.

Daryl did not manage to turn her attempt against her, but he did get out of the way to turn her paralyzing attack into a minimal nuisance.

Nursing his injured knee, the vampire did not bother to stand. He swiped Turquoise's back leg out from under her before she had recovered her balance from the miss, and the only thing she could do was control the fall.

She let herself fall away from Daryl, so that when she landed she was the perfect distance for another kick to his already broken knee.

She turned quickly, but Daryl was quicker. Still fighting from the ground, he dragged her to him and hit her squarely across the jaw. He did not need to bother striking sensitive areas or waiting for opportunity; his strength made any blow strong enough to daze.

Turquoise turned her face away from the blow, moving with it to absorb the brunt of the force and retaliating at the same time. Sparks crossed her vision even as her attack snapped the weak floating rib off Daryl's rib cage, driving it back and causing him to release her.

He rolled away, and shoved himself up. She did the same, both of them momentarily too hurt to press an advantage.

She got to her feet first; Daryl was still struggling with his knee. He wasn't in too much of a hurry. Most vampires instinctively discounted humans as a threat, no matter how many kills a hunter had on her record or how the fight was going. Vampires were called "immortal," after all. No human could kill them.

Daryl was pushing up from his knees when Turquoise repeated her earlier attempted attack, striking his head hard and fast. She felt the impact all the way up her leg as the kick made contact, the resistance of bone that gave way with a *crunch*.

His neck snapped, and the vampire tumbled back to the ground. A broken neck is paralyzing to any creature, even one that can survive and heal the injury.

Turquoise hated running, but short of tearing Daryl's head off, she knew no way to kill a vampire without a weapon. Like most humans, she wasn't strong enough for barehanded decapitation.

But retreat chafed on her nerves. One thing Crimson always taught: eliminate your enemies. Leaving prey alive gave it a chance to recover and win the advantage next time. A second fight rarely went as well as the first.

The cougar had fled somewhere during her fight with Daryl, probably distressed to see the vampire losing. Eric was waiting for her on the other side of the iron fence.

She barely remembered scaling the fence. She remembered Eric asking if she was okay, and nodding sharply before leading the way into the forest behind Midnight. She had no idea how far away the town was, but she would not stop until they were out of Jaguar's land.

Later, she could examine the painful

swelling of her jaw. Later, she could wash and bandage the wounds from the cougar's claws. Later, she could pause to wonder what on earth she was going to do with a fourteen-year-old boy. Now, she just wanted to go to ground and disappear.

They reached town at a slow limp at about noon. Eric obviously wasn't used to so much walking, but he never complained. Turquoise's adrenaline carried her through the many miles, leaving her with the focused energy and feeling of immortality that always followed a fight. More than anything, she wanted to go back and pound the cougar, which must have called to Daryl when Jaguar did not respond to its summons.

Instead, she found a pay phone in some hole-in-the-wall town a couple miles down from the end of Jaguar's territory. The street signs declared this to be Main Street, in some town called Logging.

"Yes?" Nathaniel's faint voice over the static-filled telephone wires was the sweetest sound she had ever heard.

"It's Turquoise," she said quickly. "I need

a place to stay for a couple days where I can't be tracked."

"Until the waters cool?" Nathaniel responded. "I've got a place you can borrow. I'll lend you some cash so you don't get traced pulling out your funds. Tell me where you are and I'll pick you up."

She told him, wondering how much this was going to cost her. It didn't really matter though. She had made enough in Crimson — vampire hunting could be a lucrative business — that she could comfortably retire for the next seventy years if she wanted. Whatever price Nathaniel charged, it would be worth it.

"Wait fifteen minutes so I can make a reservation for you, and then check into the inn down the street. I'm a few hours away, so you'll have a chance to patch up and get some sleep."

Blissful advice.

"I'll see you soon," he bid her. She responded in kind, and then found the phone dead in her hand.

No barter, no price. Nathaniel was as proper a mercenary as there came, and when he made a deal, he kept it. He never forgot to include a price, but he had agreed to give his help without stating one, and couldn't change the terms later.

She would puzzle it out later. For now, she turned back to Eric. "Just a block more, and we can get some sleep."

The kid smiled. *Smiled*, after all he had been through, and despite the exhaustion that was clearly written on his features. Miracles do still happen after all.

CHAPTER 17

"CATHERINE, PUT THE BOY DOWN," Daryl commanded, "and I won't have to hurt him."

She reluctantly set Tommy down, though his small, trembling hand gripped hers tightly enough that her fingers were going numb. "Tommy, run," she commanded, pushing him away.

The boy hesitated, long enough that the creature reached forward and twined pale fingers in Tommy's soft brown hair. "You love your sister, Thomas?" the creature asked softly, kneeling so he was looking the young child in the eye.

"Let him go!" she shrieked, launching herself at the pair, trying to separate them. The creature simply glanced in her direction and backhanded her *casually, a light tap compared to what he would do later.*

He released the boy and caught Catherine's arm as she tried to hit him, brushing his fingers across her cheek. She jerked back from his touch. "Catherine—" he began, but before he could continue she lashed out, striking him in the throat with all the force of terror, hatred, and fury.

The creature cursed, releasing her, and she was off in a sprint. She had barely reached the driveway when it caught up, and a shove sent her sprawling. Her palms and knees tore open as she struck the pavement, less than a foot away from her father's body. Where was Tommy? Had he gotten away, or . . .

"Catherine." He dragged her to her feet, his grip on her wrist bruising. "Never hit me." He hit back. She tasted blood in her mouth for a moment before she fell into the encroaching darkness.

Turquoise woke to find herself coated in a sheen of cold sweat. She was lying on a bed in a room she did not know. The dream left a sour taste in her mouth, and agitation in her mind.

She sat up quickly, and was rewarded by a series of shooting pains.

Sunlight was streaming in through the nearby windows. She closed the curtains, which caused the throbbing in her head to subside a bit, and pushed her bitter history from her thoughts.

Slowly, more recent memories returned to her. Nathaniel had picked her and Eric up, and brought them here. Driving through it, the town had seemed as familiar and as alien as all small towns were to her, though she hadn't seen much before she had slept.

Turquoise stood and forced herself to stretch. She walked to Eric's room, wincing at each step she took; a glance through his partly open door revealed that he was still sleeping soundly. Then, having reassured herself that he was safe, she took a hot shower and put on clean clothes.

"Is this yours?" she had asked, when Nathaniel had handed her the key to the house.

He had nodded slightly. "I haven't stayed here in a while, though. At the moment, it belongs to this girl here," he had added, tossing her a leather wallet. Examining the contents, she had found a license with her picture on it, a platinum Visa, a bankcard, a library card, and three twenty-dollar bills. "Since you can't tap into your accounts from here without being traced, I thought you could use a new identity with access to a little cash," Nathaniel had explained. "I also took the liberty of swiping some of your clothing from your Bruja house; it's in an overnight bag in the master bedroom's closet."

She hadn't ached so much then. During her sleep, all the muscles she had abused the evening before had stiffened.

The house was a small one-story, with two bedrooms, a bathroom, a kitchen, and a wraparound porch. Though clean, it had a feeling of emptiness that their presence had not yet eased.

The kitchen had a pale blue-marble linoleum floor, dark blue counters, and pine cupboards. The refrigerator was completely empty, and warm; Turquoise had to find the plug and turn the thing on. The burners on the stove looked unused, and the cupboards were equally bare. There were no pots or pans, no silverware, no paper towels or plastic bags, no toaster, and no can opener—a vampire's house. Nathaniel didn't need to eat here.

There was, however, a phone and a phonebook. Pizza sounded like a grand breakfast. But first she had to call Nathaniel and find out what the hell was going on. She dialed his number from memory, and waited three rings before remembering that it was midmorning and Nathaniel was probably asleep.

An answering machine clicked on, and a mechanical voice informed her, *"There is no answer. Please leave a message after the tone."*

"Nathaniel, I need to talk to you. Give me a call whenever you can." She hesitated, and then awkwardly added, "Thanks," before hanging up.

Nathaniel didn't approve of thanks. He always assured his clients that he did everything for his own gain, not theirs, and that gratitude was therefore out of place. Turquoise had believed him, until today. Twice, once when he had taken her from Daryl and now with all this, Nathaniel had helped her without asking for payment.

Turquoise shook her head. He would call

or he wouldn't; until then, she might as well get settled and fed.

She didn't have long to wait before Eric emerged from his room. His stomach was rumbling as loudly as hers, and he had no objection to takeout.

"I'll go shopping sometime today," she assured him, as they munched on their cheese pizzas. "If I can find a grocery store." She frowned. "And someplace to buy silverware." Shopping was probably her least favorite thing to do. A waste of time, by her book, it was an excellent practice in tedium.

Eric nodded. "I saw a little houseware shop in town. We drove right past it. I can walk there."

Startled, Turquoise had to remind herself that Eric had been the human liaison to Jaguar's town from Midnight. He was young, and depended on others for security, but he had taken on adult responsibilities in Midnight and hadn't lost that experience now that he had left—temporarily anyway. Once Jeshickah was no longer a threat, Eric would probably want to return to Jaguar's Midnight. His life was there.

"I'll drive you," Turquoise offered. "I don't

want to split up." Eric's gaze fell, and she recognized that he was hurt. He didn't want her to treat him like a kid. "Anyway, we need too much for you to carry it all back," she assured him. He didn't look like he bought the explanation, but she couldn't soothe his ego. He didn't think like a kid, or act like a kid, but that didn't mean she felt any less protective.

Eric's houseware store proved a success; they found all they needed to stock the kitchen easily and hit the grocery store next. Turquoise wasn't a picky cook—she usually ate cereal in the mornings and something canned in the evenings—so Eric insisted he would cook. She trailed along behind, unable to stop herself from scanning the aisles as if looking for threats.

Her eye paused at a boy about her age, who looked vaguely familiar, though she couldn't place him. He was browsing the Asian specialty food section, but happened to glance at her as she passed.

The boy did a double take, and then turned. Turquoise started to fall instinctively into a fighting stance before she reminded herself that this boy was human and she was in a public area.

"Cathy?" His voice held surprise, and wonder. "I haven't seen you since . . . I guess since I went away to college. How are you?"

She looked at Eric as if for help, but he was without answer. "I'm okay," she answered vaguely. *Who was this guy?* Clearly, someone who had known her before Daryl. So many memories from that time had faded, unnaturally so. "How are you?"

"I'm okay," he answered, apparently unaware of her discomfort. "Graduated last spring. I'm a history major." He laughed. "For all the good it will do me."

History . . . yes, she vaguely recalled a friend interested in history. Oh, she did remember this guy now. She had dated him, when she had been a junior and he had been a senior. But she could not for her life remember his name.

He had been away at college on her eighteenth birthday, when all hell had entered her life.

"Where are you now?" he asked.

"What?" *Great, intelligent conversation, Turquoise.*

"You were looking at Smith when I fell off the edge of the earth," he reminded her cheerfully. "Did you end up going there?" She was spared the need to respond when the boy noticed Eric. "Is that Tommy?"

Turquoise shook her head, and her voice was just a little too sharp as she answered, "No." Seeing the boy's confusion, she lied, "He's the neighbor's kid. I'm baby-sitting for him."

"Oh. That's cool," he answered.

She had to get out of here. The last thing she ever wanted to do was chat with Greg.

Greg. That was his name. Randomly, she remembered helping him with a senior prank. They had stolen one of the dissection rats from the bio lab, put bread around it, covered it with plastic wrap, and planted it in the middle of the sandwich bar in the cafeteria. What kind of bad luck had put him into her path now?

"What are you doing here?" she asked.

The words came out a little sharp. Greg looked startled, but responded with the same light humor. "I've got an apartment in town. I know, I said I'd never live in a small town, but I guess I was wrong." He checked his watch, and winced. "I've got to go, but I'll give you a call sometime. We should get back in touch. Do you live nearby?"

Didn't he know Catherine Minate was *dead*? Her body had never been found, of course, but she was as dead as any corpse in the ground. Turquoise still had some of her memories, though all of them had faded to a frightening extent, but she was not the innocent, mischievous girl who had planned pranks and gone to parties with Greg.

"I'm in town, but I just moved in.... I don't know the number." That at least was honest. *Please, leave me alone*, she added mentally. If she hadn't been worried about running into him again, as she was likely to do if they were living in the same small town, she would have lied.

She did not know why she felt the incredibly strong desire to run, but at the moment, she wanted to flee from this specter of her past.

"Oh, well, my apartment should be in the phone book," Greg said, undaunted. More quietly, he added, "I've missed you, Cathy."

So have I, Turquoise thought. She missed Cathy Minate more than anyone else could.

"I'll see you around," she said as Greg hoisted his basket of groceries.

"Yeah, I'll see you."

She fled the aisle as soon as he had turned away. Quickly Eric finished shopping, and just as quickly they paid and hurried to Turquoise's car.

"So who was that?" Eric asked.

"An old friend," Turquoise answered vaguely. She looked at the store, but could not see Greg from where they were parked.

Eric turned toward her with worry drawn on his face. "He talked like you two were close."

"He and Cathy were close," Turquoise amended.

Eric frowned. "Aren't you Cathy?"

"No," Turquoise argued. "Cathy was . . . stupid. She couldn't defend herself. Blissfully ignorant," she added dryly.

"Innocent. Not stupid."

"What makes you so wise?" Turquoise grumbled, mostly to herself. She started the car, attempting to drop the conversation.

Eric wouldn't let it drop; he answered her question. "It's the same thing the vampires do," he answered, "and I've spent a lot of time around them. You don't want to think of Cathy as you because she had weaknesses. You're a hunter, so you're not allowed to have weaknesses. A predator doesn't like to admit it's ever possible it can be prey." Quietly, he added, "And maybe you don't want to think that the girl Greg dated was capable of killing."

Turquoise realized her knuckles were white from gripping the steering wheel too hard. She bit back a sharp criticism, remembering at the last moment that she had agreed to bring him, and had not been forced into it. "Cathy couldn't make herself crush a spider walking on her bedside table," she argued, her voice tight. "She *was* weak, and Daryl destroyed her."

"Cathy is *you*," Eric asserted again. "Daryl couldn't destroy her. He just made her a little harder, a little more scared—yes, scared," he continued, ignoring Turquoise's protest. "Cathy didn't need to hunt because she wasn't afraid of life."

"Okay, then I'm scared," Turquoise growled. "But I can't go back. I know what's out there, and if I turn my back on it, that won't make it disappear."

"You'd rather admit Daryl won than admit you were ever prey," Eric said softly.

"Daryl *did* win—that battle." She was nearly shouting now. "He murdered my father and my ten-year-old brother in front of me, and I couldn't save them. I couldn't fight him. I couldn't do anything. I spent one year in his house, little better than a pet, and I couldn't do anything about it. Cathy died in there—her innocence, her illusions, her dreams—"

"Your dreams," Eric interrupted. "What are you now? A hunter; I know that. Anything else?"

The question stymied her. Anything else?

Turquoise Draka was a high-ranking member of Crimson, and one of two competitors for the position of leader. She had a web of contacts and associates, but friends? Those were scarce, if they existed at all. She had a love of the hunt, an addiction to the sweet rush of adrenaline. Anything else?

Probably another ten or fifteen years of life. Though the lifespan of a member of Bruja was slightly longer, most hunters didn't live past their mid-thirties. Age could catch up, making the hunter slow. But mostly death came in the form of the inevitable slipup. Carelessness. Human imperfection.

"Let it drop, Eric," she ordered, or tried to. Her voice wasn't hard enough to be commanding.

"What did Cathy want to do?" Eric pressed, his voice more gentle now.

"I said, let it drop."

Cathy had wanted to help people. She had wanted to go into medicine, or teaching. She had wanted to work with children; Turquoise remembered that. She had cared about everything.

And everything had been able to hurt her.

Some people use things—people, objects. They destroy. You're a creator, a builder, a healer, not a user. That line came to her mind time and again, no matter how wrong it now was.

Now she was a killer, a mercenary. And that was all.

CHAPTER 18

NATHANIEL WAS WAITING in her living room when she got home. Lounging on the couch in jeans, a T-shirt, and a denim jacket, he looked casual and chic at the same time. Moreover, he looked comfortable, as if brightly lit suburban homes were a natural part of his life.

He rose to his feet like a cat, in one smooth movement, to greet them. "Eric, it's good to see you safe. Milady Turquoise, you look like he's been tugging your chain."

"A bit." Turquoise worked to wipe the frown from her brow.

Eric looked between the two of them, and

then announced, "I'm going to put stuff away."

"I can help—"

He shook off her offer. "No problem."

"That boy is about a hundred years old," Turquoise sighed.

"Too much time around vampires," Nathaniel agreed. "He's not worse off than you are, though." In response to her wary expression, he added, "I've no plan to chastise you. Your life is your own."

Not wanting to dwell, Turquoise broke right into her questions. "Did I get set up for a suicide mission?"

Nathaniel sat back down. "If you were after Jeshickah, yes. There are vampires thousands of years older than she is that would love to destroy her, but know better than to put the knife in place themselves."

"Why? She isn't so strong," Turquoise asserted. "A knife in her heart would kill her. Who's protecting her that can make other vampires wary?"

"Jeshickah's sister is one of Siete's fledglings." Seeing Turquoise's confusion, he elaborated, "Siete is the creature that created our kind. He's ancient; people say he's truly immortal. If you killed Jeshickah, her sister would demand your death, and Siete isn't a creature you could fight." He shook his head. "When you asked to get into Midnight, I'd thought you were after Jaguar. If I had known who your target was, I would have stopped you."

"Why?" she pressed. "I've never known you to watch out for anyone else, not unless you were paid for it. Why now?"

"This might surprise you," Nathaniel retorted, and Turquoise realized suddenly that she had insulted him, "but I was human for twenty years before I was changed, and unlike some of Jeshickah's fledglings, I actually had a soul. I consider you a friend, Turquoise. Is it so shocking that I wouldn't want you to die?"

No words came to Turquoise's lips. Completely taken aback by his revelation, she could only shake her head.

"I was one of her early experiments," Nathaniel explained. "Her third fledgling. She intended for me to be a trainer; I was the first person to refuse her and survive." His gaze flickered to the kitchen, where Eric was busy ignoring them, and then returned to

Turquoise. "After me, she started looking for those who already showed the tendencies she wanted. Gabriel was her favorite, but she was too fond of him; she never managed to own him, not the way she did the others.

"The others, of course, included Jaguar."

A moment of silence passed before Turquoise ventured, "But why, however many years later, did you save me from Daryl? You're not evil, but you say it yourself—you're no white knight."

"I don't know." He shook his head. "Daryl wanted to get rid of you anyway, so it was no skin off my back. And maybe because you reminded me of myself."

"Of you?" The words came out a startled yelp.

"When I was a human," he clarified, "in Jeshickah's Midnight."

Turquoise stood, too frustrated to stay still. "You were another one of her . . . pets?"

"Never," he quickly replied. "She tried. She lost her temper before she broke me, and she hurt me too badly for me to survive as a human. She preferred to change me rather than admit defeat, and by the time she realized she couldn't control me, I was too influential in her empire for her to destroy me." He continued before Turquoise could respond. "It sounds like Jaguar has experienced the same sense of familiarity with you," Nathaniel added.

"You, I could believe," Turquoise retorted. "But I've heard enough about Jaguar's life to know we have nothing in common. Cathy had a perfect life before Daryl took her." She could hear the bitterness in her voice. She had spent eighteen years as a blissful innocent before being thrown abruptly into pain. She had barely survived the break.

Would she rather have had Jaguar's life? She had lost everything to Daryl, but at least she had good memories, faded as they were.

Nathaniel shook his head. "Jaguar's trying to break away from Jeshickah. He won't be able to do that until she's dead, and even then I doubt he'll ever fully manage it. You're trying to break away from Daryl—"

"I *have*," Turquoise corrected.

Nathaniel just nodded, and tactfully changed the subject. "What's your plan now?"

"I don't have one," she answered honestly.

"Are you going back to Bruja?"

"Of course. I've got Challenge to fight," she responded immediately, though the moment she said the words she wondered about them. Eric's questions about Cathy's dreams fluttered around in her brain, brushing uncomfortably against her thoughts.

Nathaniel had introduced her to Bruja. She had entered the guild as a chance to get strong, and to learn to defend herself. She had not intended for it to be her whole life, but hunting had consumed her. What else was she supposed to do? Sitting in classrooms didn't strike her as something she could survive. Chatting with Greg had given her a good idea of how distant her life was now from the one she had once planned.

Nathaniel sensed her uneasiness, and turned the conversation from personal to general. "They say one of the original founders of Bruja was a vampire."

"It wouldn't surprise me," Turquoise answered. "The guilds aren't known for their humanity. Is the vampire still . . . alive?" It seemed strange, asking if a vampire was alive, but English didn't have a better word.

"She's alive," Nathaniel answered. His voice was light, almost humorous. "But she refuses to answer whether the rumor is true. She alternates between living as a reclusive artist, and cutting an unmerciful, bloody swath through human society. Everyone needs balance, I suppose."

Turquoise chuckled, imagining the contrast.

Nathaniel's expression clouded; he reached into his jacket pocket for something. "Jaguar suspected you would be in contact with me. He wanted me to give you this." Reluctantly, he handed over a sealed letter.

"Have you read it?" Just because the letter was sealed didn't mean Nathaniel hadn't opened it.

"Jaguar paid me well," Nathaniel replied. "He's worked with enough mercenaries to mention I wasn't allowed to read it." If Jaguar hadn't specifically included that clause, Nathaniel would have broken the seal without hesitation. A major part of his business was information.

On the flip side, if Nathaniel took money for his client's confidentiality, he would never violate it.

As Turquoise slit the envelope, Nathaniel added, "He's trying to respect your wish for privacy, but if you really don't want him to know where you are, you have to get rid of the boy." Turquoise's gaze lifted in an involuntary glare, in response to which Nathaniel flashed a harmless smile. She had agreed to take care of Eric; she wouldn't ditch him. "I had a feeling you wouldn't go for it. But the kid belongs to Jaguar. Any trainer can track his slaves, no matter where they go."

She absorbed the information as she read the short note Jaguar had written, which invited her to meet him at a place of her choosing, at a time of her choosing. She could send an answer via Nathaniel.

What did she have to lose? She wanted to know what was happening with Jeshickah, and when Eric could safely return to the place he considered his home.

Honestly, she admitted to herself that she also missed Jaguar. He had been a rare curiosity, a splash of warmth and sincerity after two years in the cold darkness of a hunter's life. Even embroiled in all the power struggles and chaos of his world, Jaguar had a kind of wistful innocence that Turquoise could not help but envy.

Besides, a little companionship would be

nice. Greg was sweet, and she was sure he would be willing to fill the empty hours she had on her hands, but it was hard to imagine a close friendship with him. He didn't know, couldn't know, what her life was like. How close could she get to someone who didn't even know the monsters existed, after she had fought them tooth and nail for her very sanity?

She invited Jaguar to meet her in a café in the town center.

"I've told you before, you're mad," Nathaniel informed her, as he took the message. "But it's never seemed to change your mind."

CHAPTER 19

JAGUAR SHOWED UP exactly on time. Turquoise blinked at her first glimpse of him in the doorway, trying to assure herself it was really the vampire she knew.

Jaguar would attract eyes everywhere he went; he would never be able to blend into a small town. But he was trying.

His hair had been brushed back from his face and tied, so from the front it appeared short. He was wearing jeans; that alone was weird. They were black, faded a bit at the knees, but seeing Jaguar in denim was a shock. He was also wearing a very simple dark green T-shirt. Turquoise had grown so used to seeing bare caramel skin that he looked odd fully dressed.

He could pass for human. When he tried, he could look almost normal. If they had been in any city, no one would have looked twice at him.

"You're looking . . . bland." The words were out of her mouth before she could consider them.

Jaguar laughed, sliding into the seat opposite her. "I could veil the mind of every human in here so they wouldn't notice me, but it requires more concentration than I feel like expending."

"You're getting stares, anyway," Turquoise pointed out, nodding toward a teenage girl a few tables away.

Jaguar glanced at the girl, who suddenly turned back to her food as if she had forgotten Jaguar was present. The brief display of power was unnerving.

"Man of many talents," Turquoise murmured.

"And I'll admit to at least half of them," he quipped.

Since she knew Nathaniel's words would eat at her thoughts until she had the answer, she ventured, "Nathaniel said something about your being able to track Eric if you wanted to. That another of your talents?" At Jaguar's nod, she asked, "How?"

"Eric's mine," he answered, as if that explained it. Turquoise's confusion must have showed, because he elaborated, "The connection's not as strong as a blood bond, but I recognize his mind, and I can find it if I look. I don't work as a trainer anymore, so I don't usually take advantage of the bond, but it's still a habit to make the connection with any mind not strong enough to lock me out."

Turquoise remembered with distinct disquiet the times when Jaguar's mind had brushed hers. "Does that include me?"

"You put up walls that keep everyone out," Jaguar answered. The lack of a yes or a no made Turquoise uneasy. "You've dropped them around me before. I try not to take advantage of people who trust me—they're rare enough as it is."

Trust was an almost obscene word inside the mercenary world; it meant you were always susceptible to betrayal. Turquoise was struck with the desire to argue with Jaguar as soon as he spoke the word, but he was right. She *did* trust him, to the point where she had not even flinched for a knife when she had seen him. She had taken him at his word that he meant her no harm in this visit.

Jaguar changed the subject. "You might like to know Jeshickah will be out of the way very soon. There's a Triste by the name of Jesse who seems to think he has enough allies of his own to risk offending hers, and is willing to deal with her for a highly exorbitant price." Tristes had the strengths of vampires and witches combined, as well as blood that was deadly to any vampire that tried to feed on them. It made them the perfect vampire hunters.

"How long will this take?" Turquoise asked. Vampires often judged time differently than humans did.

"A few weeks, maybe a month," Jaguar answered.

"I assume then Eric will be able to go back safely?"

"He may be a kid, but he did a lot of work there; it's chaos without him," Jaguar admitted. "You'll be welcome back once she's gone, too," he ventured. "Not as a slave. Just a guest. Or, if you ever get bored with Bruja, the town of Pyrige has plenty of spaces for people willing to work."

"I'll consider it." She shrugged. "What's happening with Ravyn?"

"She's living it up, enjoying abusing Gabriel's power. It's more likely she'll enslave him than the other way around." He smiled wryly. "Gabriel has a fondness for women who are willing to kill him; it's a dangerous habit of his."

"And yours," Turquoise observed.

Jaguar paused for a reflective moment. "I like to think you would at least hesitate before trying to kill me. If I'm wrong, kindly don't correct me. I enjoy my illusions," he added, attempting to lighten the mood. "Ravyn said something about hoping you still plan to show up for Challenge?" His tone made the words a question.

"Ravyn and I are rivals. Challenge will determine who gets to lead Crimson. If I don't show, Ravyn gets the title." She was about to add, *"If I do show, she'll beat me, then get the title,"* when she remembered who she was talking to. "Would you like to help me practice?"

"What's the weapon?"

"Whip."

He looked intrigued. "You know how to use one?"

"Just barely."

Jaguar shrugged. "There's not much time, but I'll teach what I can. Maybe you'll turn out to have a knack for it."

"Or maybe I'll take out my own eye," Turquoise retorted. In a way, she hoped she would lose miserably, and have an excuse to quit Bruja. Recent events had given her too much doubt.

As always, Jaguar was painfully astute. "Do you want to win?"

"Yes." After a moment, she changed her answer to, "I don't want to lose to Ravyn. I'm just not sure I want the title."

Jaguar nodded. "There's something that might help you make your choice," he informed her. "Ravyn's worried you'll chicken out of Challenge, so she made a deal with Gabriel. He bought you from Jeshickah; if you win at Challenge, he'll make you legally freeblood."

Turquoise frowned. "I'm free now. I don't care about the legalities."

"Maybe not," Jaguar acknowledged, "but

if you want to work in our world you will."
He continued, "Shape-shifters and witches
are born free. Only their own kind can sell
them to Midnight. Humans don't have that
protection; any vampire can pick them up
and claim them, just like Daryl did with
you."

"And if I take this title Gabriel is offering?"

"Freeblood means you'll be treated like
one of us. It doesn't mean no one's allowed to
kill you, but it does mean none of us can
claim you. It means the next time you work
with our mercenaries, you don't have to
worry about having someone like Daryl pay
them to turn you over instead of helping you.
And it means that you can walk into Midnight and even Jeshickah wouldn't be able
to break you."

"And if I kill Daryl?"

"I'm not going to stop you," Jaguar answered. "Neither will Gabriel. Jeshickah
might cause some trouble, but she isn't fond
of him either, and she'll be out of the picture
soon anyway."

"And then . . . what if I said that I wanted
to give up Bruja?"

Jaguar appeared skeptical. "You can't go

back to what you were before Daryl. You're still human by blood, but in your mind and in your soul you're no more human than most of the vampires I know."

Turquoise responded flippantly, "Maybe I can't go back. But what's the other choice? Ask you to open a vein so we fix that little problem of blood?"

She had not considered the words, but once spoken they did not surprise her. If she wouldn't stay in the twilight, and she couldn't go back to Cathy's daylight world, then of course, vampire blood would be the only choice.

Voice cool and level, Jaguar answered, "It's a viable choice, but not from me. Find someone who's freeblood if that's what you want—your mercenary friend Nathaniel, for example. He didn't hesitate to burn Midnight the first time, or to sell two hunters into it. I'm sure he wouldn't have any scruples about giving one of Bruja's best immortality. And get rid of Daryl first. He might have no legal claim over you, but you don't want him arguing ownership for the next millennium."

Turquoise had hunted vampires for two

years. The idea of becoming one of them should have been sickening.

Should have been. She found herself contemplating it for a moment.

"I don't know," she said. She seemed to be saying that a lot lately.

"Go to Challenge," Jaguar recommended. "Win. Then decide. If you decide to become one of us, you'll be strong. If you don't, you'll still be able to survive."

Turquoise nodded, taking the advice. Face Challenge now; save the future for tomorrow.

Jaguar frowned, looking past her, then spoke quietly. "I think this one is looking for you."

Turquoise turned, following Jaguar's gaze, and ended up looking at Greg.

The human's gaze was resting on Jaguar with what wasn't exactly anger, but wasn't warm fuzzy friendship, either. He looked away from the vampire to greet Turquoise, but his proverbial hackles were up.

"Cathy, hey." He glanced at Jaguar again, and seemed to decide to be polite. "I noticed you and figured I'd swing inside for a moment. Am I interrupting?"

Flustered, Turquoise looked between the two, caught briefly in a hazy shadow. Greg and Jaguar didn't belong in the same world.

Jaguar covered for her, standing and offering his hand. "I'm Kyle Lostry, one of Cathy's friends." Having Jaguar use her childhood nickname struck her in a most unpleasant way.

Greg banked his hostility, and accepted Jaguar's gesture of civilized greeting like someone who had never been lied to or manipulated, someone who expected sincerity. "Greg Martin. I knew Cathy in school," he offered, looking to Turquoise, "but we've been out of touch for a while." He backed off, aware enough to sense awkwardness. "I've got to get going; I'm on my way to a job interview." He looked at Turquoise, and the expression on his face was honest, unschooled. "Give me a call?"

"I will."

Watching his back as he left, she knew she would. To forestall Jaguar's questions, she asked, "Who's Kyle Lostry?"

Jaguar looked startled, as if he had not thought about the name when he had used it.

"Someone I knew once—and wish I'd had a chance to know better."

She sensed that there was a story behind the words. "Is he . . ." She broke off, not wanting to ask whether this phantom was alive or dead.

Jaguar volunteered no more. "Is your Greg why you're thinking of leaving Bruja?" he asked. Turquoise couldn't tell from his tone or expression what he thought of Greg, or the idea.

She shook her head. "I ran into him yesterday. He somehow managed to remind me of all the things I left behind, after Daryl. . . ." She trailed off. "I don't know whether I could still follow any of those dreams, or whether I would still want to, but it hurts to know I threw them away."

Jaguar was still watching Greg, who had paused on the sidewalk to talk to someone else. "He's too innocent for you. His life is too innocent for you."

"I know."

Jaguar shook his head. "I've never known anyone who joined our world and then managed to go back to the human one." Turquoise could see in him the same longing she had once seen as he watched Shayla, and could tell he had tried. "You could thrive in my world; darkness suits you. But if you want it, Greg's world—the world his Cathy came from—might still be worth fighting for."

CHAPTER 20

DURING THE NEXT MONTH, Turquoise's days and evenings became an interesting study in contrasts.

Her mornings were usually domestic. She or Eric would make breakfast and eat together. A couple of times Greg joined them. Turquoise tried valiantly to bridge the gap to the human's world. He thought she was a freelancer for a small newspaper, a lie that seemed to work well enough. He also thought she was dating Jaguar, a.k.a. Kyle Lostry. The lies were imperfect, but at least it kept him from getting the wrong impression. She could handle having Cathy's old

boyfriend as a friend, but she quickly realized that they would never be as close as
they once were. There was too much of her
life she could never share with him. The mis-
chief they had planned together and the
dates they had gone on were still bright spots
of humor and happiness in his mind,
whereas Turquoise remembered them as if
they were faded black and white photos.
Someone else's memories, from someone
else's life.

In the afternoons, Jaguar came over, and
they practiced until midnight every night.
During their breaks, Jaguar would fill her in
on what was going on in Midnight, and in
his town. The owner of the town's only inn
had decided to elope with a young woman he
had met on vacation, and the building, one of
the few remaining properties Jaguar had not
owned, had gone up for sale; now he was just
looking for someone to manage it. He was
less than subtle in suggesting that Turquoise
could have the position, if she wanted it. She
dodged him and they went back to practice.

The owner of the local community recre-
ation center wanted to start a course in self-
defense for teenagers, and was looking for an

assistant. The job sounded more up Turquoise's alley, but she still shook her head. Challenge first. Then she planned to kill Daryl. Then she would see to the future.

Over the weeks of practice, Turquoise's own whip had given her almost as many bruises as Daryl ever had, before she had gotten the knack of it and learned not to hit herself. She was lucky Jaguar had amazing reflexes, or she probably would have taken out her own eye more than once.

She and Jaguar dueled occasionally. She used every move, piece of furniture, and dirty trick she could think of, and he kept most of his talent in check to avoid giving her more welts than she cared to receive.

At first she was hesitant to really fight, but Jaguar had offered no mercy until he was sure she was using her full force. He would heal from any wound she managed to give him, but if she got used to trying not to hurt her opponent, the habit would cripple her in a confrontation.

That was not to say Jaguar ever allowed her to hit him. Mostly he managed to evade her blows, recognizing from her form which direction the weapon would move and where it would land. Occasionally he used his own whip to catch hers, snagging the weapon out of her hand until she learned not to relinquish her hold on it.

Two quick snaps from Jaguar, and Turquoise found an X cut neatly into the stomach of her shirt.

"Careless," Jaguar chastised. She had tried an overhand snap, which left her mid and lower body unprotected, while Jaguar was in a position to attack the vulnerable area. "Do you need a break? It's late."

Turquoise took the opportunity, and faked a setup for a low crack. Jaguar moved to avoid the blow, and she brought the movement around a full circle to strike high. It had taken her days to get over her desire to wince at doing so, but she checked none of her ability; the blow landed home, and cut open Jaguar's skin.

He ignored the injury, which healed too quickly to even bleed, and soon they were again engaged in a no-mercy duel.

It was well past midnight when they finally took a break, and collapsed onto the dew-dampened grass.

Turquoise's gaze alit on the nearly full moon. Another few days, and she would have her chance to beat Ravyn in the Challenge rematch for leader of Crimson—and she *could* beat the other hunter. She had been practicing with an expert, and had no doubts as to her skills.

She just didn't know if she wanted to.

She was getting used to companionship. Eric's company was always entertaining. She enjoyed having him there for her noontime breakfast, and chatting with him during the day. He liked cooking, and she well-appreciated having dinner made for her; cleaning up afterward was a small price to pay. While domestic chores such as shopping and laundry were dreadfully dull, she was getting into the habit of seeing people.

And as annoying as it could sometimes get to discuss college, work, the news, and whatever else was on the all-too-human young man's mind, she was even getting used to Greg. His conversations were about normal, innocent life; it was so exotic to her that she could listen to what would otherwise have been dull chatter for hours.

But she couldn't juggle the two lives forever. As fond as she was becoming of her suburban life, she could not ignore what she knew. A human life would never completely suit her, because most humans would deem her mad if she tried to confide even the smallest hint of her past. And, "Yes, I work nights as a vampire hunter," usually wasn't a good line to make new friends with.

Maybe Cathy wasn't dead, but she had grown. Turquoise couldn't fit into that old life. Besides, as fond as she was of having companions, sitting around in suburbs was making her gray matter go stagnant. She needed challenge; a break was nice now and then, but boredom was not a state she would tolerate for long.

Save tomorrow for tomorrow. Deal with now first.

CHAPTER 21

THE BRUJA HALL was not imposing from the outside. Anyone looking at its exterior would see nothing more important than a redbrick house with black trim and white shutters that were always latched.

A phrase was written in Latin beside the door. Translated, it meant, "Enter the den of the hunters."

The door was unlocked, and Turquoise opened it, stepping forward into the main room of the Bruja hall with Ravyn and, strangely enough, Gabriel at her back. He confirmed Jaguar's message about the deal

Ravyn had made: legal freeblood status to the hunter who won today.

The floor was black marble, with Bruja's motto carved into it. The light was too dim for Turquoise to read it, but she knew the words by heart: *In this world, there are predators and there are prey; only the former survive.*

Turquoise entered the hall knowing she didn't want to lead these hunters.

However, she knew from experience that when a vampire involved in the trade made a deal, his word was as good as law. When Turquoise won against Ravyn today, the burgundy hunter's blood would buy her opponent's freedom. Then Turquoise could kill Daryl without worrying about whether Jaguar had gotten rid of Jeshickah yet. Then she could get on with her life.

As soon as they entered, Sarta approached. "Ravyn, Turquoise? Are you ready?"

Ravyn walked toward Turquoise, a graceful predator's walk. She snapped her whip, and it cracked little more than an inch from Turquoise's skin, then wrapped around the hunter's throat harmlessly. "I'm ready when she is."

Turquoise shook Ravyn's whip from her neck and lashed out, catching the handle of the other hunter's weapon. One quick tug before Ravyn could react, and Turquoise caught Ravyn's whip as it jerked from the woman's grip.

Sounding amused, Sarta simply said, "The fight is to third blood. Ravyn Aniketos and Turquoise Draka, you may begin."

Turquoise tossed the whip back to Ravyn, who accepted it with a glare, and the duel began.

Ravyn lazily snapped her whip in Turquoise's direction, though Turquoise had already put herself out of reach. She was testing her opponent's reflexes.

The opponents circled each other on the cold Bruja floor, watching each other for weaknesses.

"You're not going to win," Ravyn said.

Meanwhile, Turquoise watched Ravyn's arm carefully, waiting for telltale signs that the hunter was about to move. The muscles tensed.

Turquoise saw the movement before Ravyn actually attacked with the whip, and raised her own. The two leather braids twined around each other. Ravyn pulled hers away with a practiced flourish, and then attacked low.

The material of Turquoise's pant slit, but the blow wasn't hard enough to draw blood.

"Are you playing with me, Ravyn?" she asked. Turquoise flicked her own whip, which cut open the stomach of Ravyn's shirt, and Ravyn jumped back a pace. The wound did not bleed, but she could have made it do so if she had wanted. Turquoise saw the unease that slid behind Ravyn's eyes as she realized her opponent had more skill than she had suspected.

Ravyn masked the emotion. "And here I thought you had no taste for fun," she teased. This time when her whip cracked, it fell where Turquoise's left cheek should have been. Turquoise ducked out of the way, cracking her own whip as she moved.

"You little brat!" Ravyn's free hand went to the new cut on her weapon arm.

"First blood, Ravyn," Turquoise said calmly, hyper-focused.

Ravyn's whip came down hard, too fast for Turquoise to get out of the way, and landed on Turquoise's left shoulder at the hardest part of the snap. The skin split.

"First blood, Turquoise," Ravyn said sweetly. "I saw Daryl a day ago," she commented. "He gave me some pointers."

Turquoise let the barb bounce off her ears. Ravyn's whip cracked again. Turquoise moved slightly, and her opponent's whip wrapped tightly around the handle of her own. Yanking, Turquoise pulled the other hunter off balance. Before even bothering to untangle the two weapons, she flicked her own, and it cut open the back of Ravyn's left shoulder. Second blood.

Ravyn rotated the shoulder that had just been hit, and pulled her weapon away as she again moved back to gain distance.

"A little more practice, Turquoise, and you could be quite good at this," she encouraged. Ravyn liked the sound of her own voice, apparently. Turquoise personally preferred a silent fight, but many hunters liked to talk; it helped them focus, and their opponents were more likely to be distracted by engaging in dialogue.

Turquoise refused to banter, and attacked again.

Her strike fell short, but she managed to evade Ravyn's next one. There was blood running down her back from the wound on her shoulder. It wouldn't be fatal, but Turquoise was annoyed to realize that she would have yet another scar.

Ravyn sidestepped Turquoise's next attack. Her whip hit Turquoise's right wrist and snapped around it, a mirror to the blow that Lord Daryl had given her years ago.

She hissed in pain, but forced herself to keep hold of the whip. Her wrist was bleeding heavily. This fight would be over soon.

They were both at second blood. Whoever hit next would be the winner.

Ravyn attacked again, and Turquoise collapsed to the ground to dodge. Then, before the other hunter could react, Turquoise snapped her whip around Ravyn's ankle and yanked as hard as she could.

Ravyn lost her balance and fell to the floor hard on her back. Before she could recover, Turquoise struck with the whip one more time, drawing a fine band of blood from Ravyn's left cheek.

"Third blood," Turquoise announced, rising to her feet. The movement was more painful than she would have expected.

Ravyn silently raised a hand to the mark on her cheek. "If this scars, I am going to be *really* angry," she snapped as she pulled herself off the floor. "Cheap trick, Turquoise."

"It worked."

Sarta had come to Turquoise's side, and started to wrap a bandage around her wrist wound to stop its bleeding.

"Congratulations, Turquoise," she began, but Turquoise shook her off, and wrapped the bandage by herself.

"I hope Daryl snaps your neck," Ravyn growled.

With a chuckle, Gabriel wrapped an arm around his burgundy-haired friend's waist, pulling her away before she could attack her bleeding adversary. The vampire turned Ravyn toward himself, and licked the blood from her cheek.

Ravyn shoved him away.

Gabriel laughed again. He caught the hunter's wrist, and again drew her toward himself. He licked the blood from her arm, and Turquoise saw Sarta shake her head in disgust. To Turquoise, Gabriel said simply, "You're freeblood, Turquoise. Go put a knife in Daryl for me."

Ravyn leveled her garnet eyes in Turquoise's direction.

Turquoise tossed the whip down at the burgundy hunter's feet. "Take the title, Ravyn. I don't want it." She saw the shock on Ravyn's face, but did not bother to stay and explain her decision.

She didn't want to be leader of Crimson.

She ducked Ravyn's punch, and ignored the ungrateful threat, then walked out of the Bruja hall for perhaps the last time.

CHAPTER 22

THE BUS RIDE HOME —to Nathaniel's house, Turquoise hastily amended—was painfully long, and stifling. She wished she had driven, but had not wanted to risk needing to drive home injured. With a light jacket on over the black tank top she had worn to Challenge, Turquoise could feel sweat dripping down her spine. The wound on her shoulder ached as the salt found its way beneath the bandages.

She gave in, and took her jacket off, trying fiercely to ignore the looks people gave her. Maybe it was the wildly tousled hair, or the adrenaline-induced flush to her cheeks that made them stare. Or maybe it was the fact that the bandage on her wrist was highly visible.

She decided she didn't care. None of these people knew her, or wanted to know her. They weren't concerned enough to question a stranger.

Now what? she wondered. She was through with Bruja. She would need to kill Daryl eventually. His pride wouldn't allow him to ignore her forever, and even if she had been willing to hide from him—which she wasn't—he worked with mercenaries even more than she did, and would be able to track her down eventually.

What else? Eric's words echoed in her mind.

She needed action, movement, adrenaline. A tame white-picket-fence life would never suit her; it would bore her to death. She also didn't want to ditch Jaguar and Eric now. With Jeshickah out of the way, Midnight might even prove interesting for a while.

For a while. But forever? For as long as a vampire could live? She didn't know.

The bus stop was about a mile from Nathaniel's house, in the center of town.

Turquoise would have to walk home, but the day was beautiful and she had plenty of energy.

Hearing her stomach rumble, she took a detour into a gas station convenience store. She slipped her hand into her pants pocket, double-checking to make sure she had enough cash on her for some donuts and a soda. The thought amused her. She had eaten the same fare on her way to Midnight.

"Are you okay?" The old man at the register asked, a worried frown on his face as Turquoise approached to buy her snack.

Turquoise could not conceal her surprise. She had forgotten to put her jacket back on and her battered body was visible. As long as she had been in Bruja, she had stuck to anonymous cities. No one asked questions. But this town was so small and she had chatted with this man on a couple of occasions in the last month. He would know that something was wrong, and feel comfortable enough to ask.

"Yeah . . . had a fall." As a lie, it was awful.

An awkward moment ensued. The old man's eyes were questioning.

"I'm a little accident prone," she lied, trying to make the words sound realistic when they made almost no sense. She added, "I fell off a table when I was little, into a window." She tried to add a smile and a bit of a "no big deal" laugh as she said it, but the memory was too raw. Vividly she remembered catching her father's arm as Daryl shoved him back through the window. Daryl had grabbed her and tossed her onto a table, where broken glass had sliced open her arms and the backs of her shoulders.

The old man looked unconvinced. He patted her hand sympathetically as she handed him the money for her purchases. He handed her change, with a "Have a good day" good-bye.

She left quickly. Where was her jacket? She swore as she realized she must have left it on the bus.

She swore again when she recognized Greg a block down the street, walking toward her. She considered ducking back into the convenience store, but didn't want to face the old man's silent questions.

Too late anyway. Greg saw her, and waved hello, then sped up his pace to meet her.

"Cathy, hi. I . . ." He broke off, his light jog turning to a sprint as he hurried to her side. "What happened to you? Are you okay?" Then he seemed to notice that most of the scars were years old, and his eyes widened more. "What the hell? I mean, I'm sorry, but . . . what the hell?"

Turquoise's nerve ran out. She had known living here wasn't going to work from the start. She didn't have the patience to deal with him now.

"Greg, I'm a mercenary," she said coolly. "Mostly, I hunt vampires for a living. I've been debating quitting my job and teaching middle school, but I hear it's a little rough there." The words dripped with bitter sarcasm.

She knew what his reaction would be—disbelief, fear—and didn't want to see it. She pushed past him, walking quickly in the direction of her house.

Greg hurried after her, and caught her shoulder. She winced, pulling away as his touch hit the new injury.

Unsurprisingly, he was looking at her as if she had sprouted a second—no, third—head, but he *was* trying to keep up with her.

"You mean vampires like . . . um, some criminal person, right?" he said hesitantly, trying to figure out her speech. "You're a cop or something?"

He was so damn innocent. How could she ever hope to convince him?

She didn't need to. He deserved his innocence.

She backtracked, slowing her pace a bit so he could keep up. "I'm sorry. It's been a rough day," she said, stalling as she tried to add to what he already tentatively believed. If she tried, she could convince him of the reality of vampires. She could tell him what had really happened to Cathy and the rest of her family. But Greg didn't need to know. He was happy. "You know I was interested in psych, right? I got into criminal psychology in college, and I do some work with some people." She made the lies intentionally vague, as if she wasn't supposed to tell. Actually, she had no idea who she would possibly be working for; she knew nothing about the government or law enforcement. But Greg probably knew less than she did.

Greg said something noncommittal along the lines of "Uh-huh." He kept walking with her, not talking for a bit, as if digesting what he had heard.

Humans had an instinctive desire to remain at the top of the food chain. Unless forced to see reality, most of them would believe almost anything before believing that vampires and other such creatures existed.

"So. You're with the government or something?"

Crimson was about the antithesis of the United States government, but Turquoise answered, "Yeah." She added, "I'm not really supposed to talk about it." That was vague enough. It would tickle his imagination, without straining against what he believed.

Greg walked her home. They didn't talk much, though occasionally Greg made some attempt to start a new conversation. Turquoise wasn't much in the mood to chat.

"Smells like someone's having a bonfire," he commented, blinking at the faint smell of smoke. "Speaking of, some friends of mine are having a picnic next weekend. Would you like to go maybe?"

He sounded so hopeful, she had to smile. She started to say no, but then changed her mind. "Sure. Why not?"

His expression lit up.

Before he could speak, the fire truck rumbled by. They both looked after it anxiously.

"I hope everything's okay," Greg said worriedly.

Turquoise picked up her pace. The smell of smoke was thicker now. A coil of fear was making its way from her stomach to her throat to choke her.

A few houses down, she began to see the flames. She sprinted, until a fireman caught her arm, pulling her back.

"Ma'am, this area isn't safe for bystanders—"

"I live here," she spat, shoving away from him. "What . . ." She broke off. *Eric? Where was Eric?* She frantically scanned the area for the boy. "My brother was here when I left. He's fourteen. Have you seen him?"

The man hesitated. "Please wait here, ma'am."

If he was hurt . . . if one hair on his head had been singed . . .

Greg caught up to her, panting and coughing around the smoke. "What caused it?" he asked instantly. "Do they know?"

"I don't even own a toaster," Turquoise

growled back. Faulty wiring was impossible. Nathaniel wouldn't have had a house that had been poorly made. The stove and oven were new, and Eric was too experienced a cook to ever mistakenly leave one on unattended. If this wasn't arson, she'd eat the cinders.

A police officer returned from the jumble of people, leading an ash-streaked Eric. The boy broke from his escort and hurried toward Turquoise.

She couldn't help herself. She pulled the boy against herself, so grateful for his safety that she didn't care about the house. Nathaniel could deal with losing a house. Turquoise could pay for a house. There was nothing in there she could not replace.

"Are you the owner?" the officer asked.

Turquoise nodded, not really paying much attention. Instead, she spoke quietly to Eric. "What caused it?"

Eric grimaced. "Your favorite vampire," he answered, under his breath so no one other than Turquoise could hear him. Greg must have picked up a word or so. The boy took a few steps back, looking awkward.

"Ms. Emerette?" Turquoise looked at the officer dumbly before remembering that the

name on her license was something
Emerette. Margot, maybe? She couldn't remember. She was glad Greg was still dealing
with his new belief that she worked for the
government, or else he might have tried to
correct it.

"Yes?"

"Would you mind coming down to the station to answer a few questions?" he asked.

"Right now?" Right now, she would
rather go kill something than talk politely
with these friendly officers. Specifically, she
wanted to deal Daryl a long, painful death
for destroying Cathy's life, for making it impossible for her to pick up where she had left
off with Greg, and most of all for frightening
her.

Greg came to her rescue. "She doesn't
need to talk now." He spoke like he knew
what he was doing. "We'll come down after
she and the kid are cleaned up, okay?"

The officer seemed to hesitate. Turquoise
offered a watery smile. "Please," she added
to Greg's words.

The man nodded finally. "I suppose there's
no hurry. I know this is going to be a difficult
time. Do you have a place to stay?"

"Yes, she does," Greg answered for her.

They walked back to Greg's car, which he had left near where he had met up with Turquoise.

"My sister's visiting, and she probably has some clothes that will fit you," Greg offered to Turquoise. "You two can come over and clean up, then figure out whether you want to talk to the police or what."

Turquoise shook her head. "I can't."

Greg didn't seem to know how to handle that one, so Turquoise didn't make him respond.

"There's something I need to deal with first," she explained. Taking Greg up on his offer would put him in danger, at least until Daryl was dead.

"How are you going to get there?" Eric asked practically, knowing that she would go to Midnight.

That was the most difficult part of her plan.

Greg was a lifesaver. He chewed his lip for a moment, and then asked, "Do you need to borrow my car?"

There is a God. She gave him a hug. "I'll be back in less than a day." She was still armed from Challenge, and she could pick up a few more weapons from her Bruja house before getting to Midnight. It was almost on the way.

"Sure," Greg answered nonchalantly. "Just be careful with her, okay?"

It was hilariously easy for Turquoise to get inside Midnight. The raven guards at the gate did not challenge her; they were too shocked that a human was willing to fight to get *into* Midnight. Her fury was visible in every movement she made, and no one approached her until she was almost to Daryl's door.

"You no longer annoy me." The voice behind her caused Turquoise to turn, a knife instantly in her hand. She hesitated upon seeing Jeshickah, willing to wait for the vampiress to either push a fight or back off.

"Always nice to gain a new friend," the hunter retorted.

"I wouldn't go that far." Jeshickah's voice was dry.

Belatedly, Turquoise informed the vampire, "Gabriel made me freeblood."

Jeshickah nodded. "I'm aware of that. His foolishness is why I am speaking to you, instead of chaining you down so I can break every one of your bones before removing your skin and making it into a nice pair of pants." Jeshickah's expression of polite amusement never left her face as she spoke.

"Pleasant image," Turquoise answered. Impatience was gnawing at her, but she was smart enough to avoid antagonizing Jeshickah by ignoring her.

"I have determined my reasons for detesting you," Jeshickah stated. "You are too like my own pets. The traits are attractive in a man I own. They are less so in a human girl."

Turquoise thought with unease back to Jaguar's words. *Jeshickah picks her trainers for physical beauty, mental acuity, moral void, and what she calls a trainer instinct—the instinct to watch a person, determine her weaknesses, and destroy her.* Surely she didn't fit that description.

"I'm not one of your pets," she argued.

"You're willing to sell yourself, your principles, for power, strength. You'll lie, manipulate, or kill for money. And may I say you are very good at it; you have my Jaguar eating out of your hand." There was bitterness in the statement. Or jealousy? Was Jeshickah jealous?

"Do you have a point?" Turquoise spoke to keep from laughing. She didn't think Jeshickah would appreciate amusement.

"Go ahead and kill Daryl if you wish," Jeshickah purred. "He's too stupid to live anyway. But then go home. Get a job, breed, do any of the tedious things humans do. Get old and gray, and stay that way. If you take vampire blood from any of my brood—either Nathaniel or Jaguar would give it to you, at your request—know that I will control you."

That sounded unpleasant.

The conversation skidded to a halt as Jaguar stepped into the hall. His step faltered as he noticed Turquoise and Jeshickah, and when he approached, he did so cautiously.

He addressed the vampiress first. "Your Triste is requesting a meeting with you."

"That creature is no end of trouble," Jeshickah grumbled.

Jaguar shrugged. "You hired him."

"There seems to be a shortage of gray matter this century." To Turquoise, she offered, "Enjoy your sortie, girl. Don't make too much of a mess."

"How long until she dies?" Turquoise

growled, as soon as the vampiress was out of the hall.

Jaguar smiled; the expression looked too wary to be hopeful. "Not long, if Jesse does his job. Jeshickah hired him for his kind's talents at restraining vampires. It's something he is very good at." The smile was gone as he asked, "You're after Daryl?"

She absently checked one of her knives. "I've waited too long already."

"You know that if you get yourself killed, I'm going to hate myself for not stopping you," he informed her.

"I'm not planning to die."

"No one ever is." He hesitated, but then turned away. Jaguar, like most of the vampires in the building, would turn his back and not hinder her, but he wouldn't help her.

She didn't want the help. This was her fight to win or lose alone.

Turquoise kept one knife in her hand as she turned the knob and entered Daryl's room. If he wasn't in, she could wait.

CHAPTER 23

NATHANIEL HAD SAID he was there to conduct business; he didn't say what type. He had seemed surprised when she, a slave, had spoken to him, but he was willing to talk.

Despite knowing what Nathaniel was and despite knowing that Lord Daryl would be furious to find someone in his home when he returned, Cathy was grateful for the vampire's companionship.

"Would you help me kill him?" she asked, in a moment of frustration.

Nathaniel looked at Cathy as if she had finally done something interesting. "Is that really a road you want to travel?" he asked.

"Is there another choice, besides dying here?"

"You could have asked for help escaping," the mercenary pointed out.

"He killed my parents and my brother," Catherine argued. "I want to see him dead."

Daryl's room in Midnight brought back unpleasant memories, even once Turquoise had assured herself that he was not in it. From the delicate glass etching on the chair, to the whip lying ominously on the cluttered desk, every object reminded the hunter of the creature she had come to kill.

Turquoise paced restlessly, waiting. She killed some time working at the tight braid of his whip with her knife, and unraveled enough to make it harmless if Daryl got his hands on it. She started to go through the desk, and found more cash than she had ever seen, then amused herself imagining a Midnight Savings Bank.

One of her Crimson knives, a slender weapon with a blade of expensive firestone, was in her hand before Daryl finished opening the door; she saw Daryl hesitate when he caught sight of her. "Catherine," he greeted her. "I thought you would find your way back here. A slave without her master is lost, after all."

"You don't seem to understand your situation," the vampire said coldly. He reached past her to shut the door she had been trying to escape through, and she recoiled from his proximity. "I own you, Catherine, as surely as I own the shirt I'm wearing, and you don't want to make me mad."

That had been her introduction to the concept that a human being could be property. The concept had been beaten into her time and again; the more she fought, the more she had been forced to realize how powerless she was.

She actually smiled at the memory. She wasn't powerless anymore. She certainly wasn't this creature's slave. "You're not my master."

"You're human, Catherine," Daryl argued. He closed the door and leaned against it, and Turquoise realized that, while she would never prove the point to him, she no longer felt the need to argue. He continued, "Ours is simply a higher race. You are a slave by blood, and that is all you can ever be."

Without words, Turquoise attacked.

Daryl was prepared for a fight this time, and he dodged her first attack easily, and then drew his own knife.

It would have been so much easier—for Turquoise, at least—if he had just tried to bleed her. Trying to kill a feeding vampire is as easy as trying to kill a blind deaf-mute.

"Revenge," Nathaniel paraphrased. "It sounds sweet, but it doesn't make for a good life."

"Maybe not, but in this case, I think I wouldn't mind it." Bravado. Did she really think he would help her? And could she really kill, even Lord Daryl?

Nathaniel drew a knife from his boot and handed it to her, handle first. "If you're willing to kill, wait to strike until he's feeding. Go for the heart—it's the only place that will be fatal."

She hesitated. Cathy wasn't a killer; violence made her stomach turn. But as her hand closed over the knife's handle her decision was made.

Daryl caught Turquoise's wrist and knocked the first knife away. Fortunately, she had others, and Turquoise's left hand was almost as good as her right. Daryl hissed in pain as the next knife raked across the skin of his chest, but a hasty block knocked the blade from its aim and kept it from piercing the rib cage.

Lord Daryl stormed back into his home, his temper already hot and looking for an outlet. He found one as soon as he saw Nathaniel waiting in his parlor.

"What is he doing here?" Lord Daryl demanded of Cathy, as if the human should have been able to make Nathaniel leave.

"I have business with you," the mercenary replied. Lord Daryl ignored him; Nathaniel leaned back against the wall to wait.

Lord Daryl pulled Cathy against himself, wrapping her hair around his fingers to yank her head to the side and bare her throat. She shivered with the pain as his fangs pierced the skin.

The knife was in her left hand. The vampire obviously didn't see it as a threat, if he noticed it at all. Across the room, she saw Nathaniel make an X over his heart, a reminder.

But she missed the heart. The blade hit a rib and skittered across his chest, and her master threw her away with a curse.

Turquoise pulled away abruptly before he could retaliate, but his grip on her wrist didn't falter. Instead, he used the hunter's momentum to throw her.

The breath hissed out of her lungs as her back slammed into the wall, and Turquoise stumbled to her knees before she could recover it.

She hit the wall hard, and fell. The next moments were unclear; she only remembered fear, pain, and anger. Because in that moment she heard a sound that had never been directed toward her before—the crack of Lord Daryl's whip.

The weapon wrapped around her wrist, tearing open the skin; he yanked her forward, and her shoulder screamed in pain, probably dislocated.

Breathing tightly past pain that seemed to pulse from her fingers to her shoulder, down her back and through her gut, she tried to move the arm, then nearly blacked out. *No, we won't be trying that again.* In all her years as a vampire hunter, she had yet to break a bone, but there was a first time for everything.

Again came the crack. This time the whip cut open a line above her left collarbone.

Desperately, she dove with the knife. Lord Daryl didn't react quickly enough to avoid the blade, but she could not reach his heart. Instead, the weapon cut into his stomach.

Lord Daryl growled a curse, and shoved her away, toward Nathaniel. She couldn't get up again. Everything was bleeding, bruised, in pain. She barely remembered hearing him order Nathaniel, "Get her out of here."

She had been lucky then to have Nathaniel to save her. This time, she had only training and her wits to help her.

Her knife was still in her hand, held by a death grip, but only because instincts died hard. Turquoise was lucky it had not sliced her open when she fell.

Daryl was already standing above her, expression unconcerned. "You can't fight me, Catherine," he said calmly, and the words ignited her rage. "I am your master, and I will be for as long as you live. Did you honestly think you were better than I am?"

"You're Catherine Miriam Minate," her father had said, after she first met Daryl, as if that explained everything. "You're proud, and you have every right to be. And no one—no one—can take that away from you unless you let them."

Turquoise answered with a single word: "Yes."

She started fighting again, this time a series of lightning thrusts and dodges that left him off guard. The knife sliced along his arm as he fumbled a block. She barely managed to dodge his blade, by stepping in closer. Her knife cut along the back of his hand, and he dropped his weapon with a hiss of pain.

"Some people only care about themselves. They use things; they destroy," Mr. Minate told his daughter. "You're ... you're a creator, a builder. A healer, not a user."

Cathy shook her dad's words of wisdom off as hokey.

Some people use things—people, objects. They destroy. Some creatures needed to abuse others in order to thrive. This one had picked the wrong life to try to steal.

"I might never have come back here," Turquoise stated, as she fought. She moved closer, and then dodged back as Daryl tried to retaliate. "But you did something very dumb." Another series of attacks, and another quick retreat. "You threatened—" She blocked a blow; the effort sent a series of black waves through her vision. "—Eric. And you tried—" He caught her around the waist, and pulled her forward. "—to ruin the life I had just barely created again." She slammed a knee up, and Daryl shoved her away with a sound of pain.

He was expecting her to fall, or at least be delayed. Instead, she instantly swung her weapon arm up, at the same time throwing her weight forward to add power to the blow.

Finally the knife found its mark, and the creature collapsed, as a marionette will when the puppeteer cuts the strings.

Turquoise nearly fell with him, but somehow managed to lean back against the wall and grit her teeth against another wave of dizziness.

"You'll do something amazing with your future," her father stated with surety. "You've got so

much passion, so much talent . . . you'll be something incredible, I'm sure."

He hadn't been talking about hunting vampires.

Funny, that wasn't what she was thinking about, either. She had two worlds to pick her future from: human and vampiric. Or both.

First, she was going to need to see a doctor. She had no illusions about what she was at the moment—human—or about how much damage she could do to herself if she didn't get to a hospital soon to get the arm set. After that . . .

You're a creator, a builder. Who knew? Maybe she could try to find that part of herself again.

Maybe she would take Jaguar's job for long enough to decide she was bored with it, and then ask Nathaniel to change her; maybe she would salvage what Daryl had tried to destroy, and realize she was content in human life.

She had choices, and if she didn't have all of eternity, she had some time. She also had freedom.

Wryly, she mused, *In the end, my father was right.*